Also by Sheila Heti

PURE COLOUR

PURE COLOUR

SHEILA HETI

FARRAR, STRAUS AND GIROUX

NEW YORK

Farrar, Straus and Giroux
120 Broadway, New York 10271

Library of Congress Cataloging-in-Publication Data
Names: Heti, Sheila, 1976– author.
Title: Pure colour / Sheila Heti.
Other titles: Pure color
Description: First edition. | New York : Farrar, Straus and Giroux, 2022.
Identifiers: LCCN 2021044055 | ISBN 9780374603946 (hardcover)
Subjects: LCGFT: Novels.
Classification: LCC PR9199.4.H48 P87 2022 | DDC 813/.6—dc23
LC record available at https://lccn.loc.gov/2021044055

Designed by Abby Kagan

Our books may be purchased in bulk for promotional, educational, or business
use. Please contact your local bookseller or the Macmillan Corporate and
Premium Sales Department at 1-800-221-7945, extension 5442, or by email at
MacmillanSpecialMarkets@macmillan.com.

www.fsgbooks.com
www.twitter.com/fsgbooks • www.facebook.com/fsgbooks

3 5 7 9 10 8 6 4 2

ONE

After God created the heavens and the earth, he stood back to contemplate creation, like a painter standing back from the canvas.

This is the moment we are living in—the moment of God standing back. Who knows how long it has been going on for? Since the beginning of time, no doubt. But how long is that? And for how much longer will it continue?

You'd think it would only last a moment, this delay of God standing back, before stepping forward again to finish the canvas, but it appears to be going on forever. But who knows how long or short this world of ours seems from the vanishing point of eternity?

Now the earth is heating up in advance of its destruction by God, who has decided that the first draft of existence contained too many flaws.

Ready to go at creation a second time, hoping to get it more right this time, God appears, splits, and manifests as three critics in the sky: a large bird who critiques from above, a large fish who critiques from the middle, and a large bear who critiques while cradling creation in its arms.

~

People born from the bird egg are interested in beauty, order, harmony and meaning. They look at nature from on high, in an abstracted way, and consider the world as if from a distance. These people are like birds soaring—flighty, fragile and strong.

People born from a fish egg appear in a flotation of jelly, and this jelly contains hundreds of thousands of eggs, where the most important thing is not any individual egg, but the condition of the many. For the fish, it's less any one individual egg that concerns them than that eggs are laid in the best conditions, where the temperature is most right, and the current most gentle, so the majority might survive. For fish, it's the collective conditions that count. A person hatched from a fish egg is concerned with fairness and justice here on earth: on humanity getting the temperature right for the many. One thousand eggs are the concern of a fish, whereas the person hatched from the egg of a bear clutches one special person close, as close as they possibly can.

A person born from a bear egg is like a child holding on to their very best doll. Bears do not have a pragmatic way of thinking, in which their favourites can be sacrificed for some higher end. They are deeply consumed with their own. Bears claim a few people to love and protect, and feel untroubled by their choice; they are turned towards those they can smell and touch.

People born from these three different eggs will never completely understand each other. They will always think that those born from a different egg have their priorities all wrong. But fish, birds and bears are all equally important in the eye of God, and it wouldn't be a better world if there were only fish in it, and it wouldn't be a better world if there were only bears. God needs creation critiqued by all three. But here on earth, it is hard to believe it: fish find the concerns of the birds superficial, while birds are made impatient by the critiques of the fish. Nothing makes a person feel like their life's work—or their self—is less seen than when it's being judged by someone from a different egg.

Yet birds should be grateful that someone is making the structural critique, so they don't have to. And fish should be grateful that someone is making the aesthetic critique, so they can focus on the structural one.

~

God is most proud of creation as an aesthetic thing. You have only to look at the exquisite harmony of sky and trees and moon and stars to see what a good job God did, aesthetically. So those born from the bird egg are the most grateful of all. Those born from the fish egg are the most upset, and those born from the bear egg aren't too happy, either.

Perhaps God shouldn't conceive of creation as an artwork, the next time around; then he will do a better job with the qualities of fairness and intimacy in our living. But is that even possible—for an artist to shape their impulse into a form which is not, in the end, an art form?

~

This particular story concerns a birdlike woman named Mira, who is torn between her love for the mysterious Annie, who seems to Mira a distant fish, and her love for her father, who appears as a warm bear.

~

The heart of the artist is a little bit hollow. The bones of the artist are a little bit hollow. The brain of the artist is a little bit hollow. But this allows them to fly. Those who aren't hatched from the bird egg might wonder why it was birds—who centre their thoughts on their own selves—who were born to give the world its metaphors, pictures and stories. Why should it have been given to the *birds*?

A bird can learn to walk on the ground like a bear, and they can spend their whole life walking—but they will never be happy this way. While a fish on the shore gasps for breath, desperate to get back to the sea.

~

How Mira would have loved to have been born of the bear egg! How she would love to be an ambassador of a simple and enduring love, down here on this earth. Yet whenever she sets her heart on such actions, they are wished for, strived for, and barely achieved. To properly love another one—this is the stumblingest part of her, the most nonsensical part, the part of her that is most scattered and always to blame.

But she shouldn't feel bad about being a bird, for how beautiful are the flowers in her window—the flowers on her windowsill, over there. How their petals and leaves make each passerby smile, that someone loves beauty and cares. Her flowers make us think of the flowers in the soul of the person who put them there. It is the flowers in the soul of the person who put them there that make us happy and enliven our hearts. The beauty of the flowers is a clue to the beauty of a human heart. They are a keyhole into a human heart.

And a fish's good act, even the smallest action, effectively done, is a glimpse into a human heart. And a glimpse into one heart is a glimpse into many. And the hopes of the bear are shared by all of humankind. And what opens one heart opens many.

Mira left home. Then she got a job at a lamp store. The lamp store sold Tiffany lamps, and other lamps made of coloured glass. Each lamp was extremely expensive. The least expensive one cost four hundred dollars. This was a month's salary for her. Every day, before they closed up for the night, Mira had to turn off every single lamp. This took about eleven minutes. Mostly she turned off lamps by pulling on little beaded cords. She had to be careful not to let the cord snap back and hit the bulb or the lamp. She had to pull the cords with a gentle sort of care. It was tedious work. Mira didn't have the morning shift. That person had to turn on the lamps. Their job was no better than hers.

Across the street there was another lighting store. Where Mira worked, it was just a lamp store, but the other store sold all sorts of fixtures, and also ceiling lights with fans attached— very modern lighting in contrast to their old-fashioned wares. People preferred the store across the street. The owner of Mira's store had just enough customers to stay in business, since most couples went across the street and spent their money on modernistic white lamps, and off-white lamps made of industrial plastic. Mira's co-workers felt sorry for themselves, and said those people had no taste. When it was time to close up shop,

Mira would see the thin man who worked across the street turning off every single light, one by one. They both had the same nightly task. Mira felt that no one in the world understood her, but she wondered if he did. Yet, embarrassed by their similarity, she avoided eye contact with him.

She felt so alone in those days. Not that she minded. It is only when you get older that everyone makes you feel bad about being alone, or implies that spending time with other people is somehow better, because it proves you to be likeable.

But being unlikeable wasn't the reason she was alone. She was alone so she could hear herself thinking. She was alone so she could hear herself living.

How did Mira find her job at the lamp store? She must have walked past it and seen a little sign. How did people find jobs back then, back before everyone knew what everyone else wanted? Little paper signs.

How did she find the room she lived in? There was probably a scrap of paper taped up somewhere, or tacked to a corkboard at a local café. The house had two bedrooms on the second floor, and a bathroom that was shared. There was a large apartment on the main floor, which was occupied by a blond-haired gay man, who came home one night all bloodied and beaten. They met by accident on the stairs, and he turned away from her, angry and shaken.

On her floor lived a lonely man about ten years older than she was, who Mira only saw twice. He was silent and shy. In their bathroom was a dirty tub, so she never took a bath, and she rarely showered. Because the man prepared his dinner in the kitchen, she bought a hot plate for her room.

Attached to her bedroom was a draughty porch with wood-slat walls and subtly distorted windows, set into all three sides. It would have been a pretty room to sit in, if the weather had been nice. But it was fall when Mira moved in, and she was gone by early spring. She kept all the books she owned on a shelf in that freezing little room. When it was time to move out, she opened the door to collect her books and found they had all moulted and their pages had gone wavy with the damp, deep cold of the winter.

Mira entered school. She was accepted into the American Academy of American Critics, at one of its international satellite schools. It wasn't so easy to get in. Everyone who wanted to be a critic applied. There were only a few spots open each year, so everyone who was accepted immediately had something to brag about. Just getting in placed a certain stamp on your personality and mind. It meant you were a cut above the rest.

The school had a large room with tables, a sort of tetrahedron-shaped room with cheap chairs made of industrial plastic, and shiny, smoke-stained walls. This was where the students hung out. There was a tiny window through which they could buy croissants and tea, and the people who worked behind the wall were rarely, if ever, seen.

In the large room, students stood on desks, declaiming. They made their pronouncements and laughed out loud, and it was the only place in the whole building where they didn't feel they were performing for their professors. It was the only place they felt free. Their vanity was just bursting at the seams! They felt it was important to hone their insights. They knew they had to develop a style of writing and thinking that could survive down through the ages, and at the same time penetrate their own generation so incisively. That was what they had entered school for—they, the elected. They believed the future would be set in the moulds that they had made. It was important to know what you thought of things—what you believed the world to be, and what you thought it *should* be.

~

They just didn't consider the fact that one day they would be walking around with phones in the future, out of which people who had far more charisma than they did would let flow an endless stream of images and words. They just had no idea that the world would become so big, or the competition so stiff.

They ate croissants and drank tisane. They smoked pot and went to class high. They had few lessons, and the ones that were offered were worthless and out of date.

Every morning, they had to practice Tai Chi in the school basement. The sessions were led by a teacher in his mid-fifties who was thin and brisk. The implication was that if they practiced Tai Chi every morning for the rest of their lives, they would turn out as energetic and capable as he. Everyone went except Matty, who didn't think that a critic needed to know Tai Chi. The very fact of the classes enraged him! He thought they should be sleeping in. He hadn't been told, upon acceptance, that performing Tai Chi at eight in the morning was the obligation of every student. If he had known, he wouldn't have applied. It was up to him if he wanted to move his body or not, and it was nobody's business but his own. Although his classmates agreed with him, they all went to Tai Chi anyway.

Mira had only been at the school for a few days when she first saw Matty coming up from the lake, where he had been bathing, naked. He saw her, nodded. She saw him, nodded back, and quickly looked away. He was tall, big, and his penis was hanging low, his scrotum was red, and he was hairy all over, and his hair was hanging low, and his lips were puffy, and his eyes were red from the water, and he looked at her in a slow way, and raised his hand to her slowly, and Mira just hoped she would not encounter him the rest of the time she was there.

Their old professor, Albert Wolff, stood before a screen on which was projected a slide of a painting of an asparagus. He made a great display of looking for what he did not see, while the students stood around him in the darkened room. He explained that the world was still going through a fashionable love of Manet, but that soon everyone would come to share his point of view.

"Édouard Manet is a curious personality. As a painter, he has an eye but no hand. The fairy godmother who presided at his birth gave him the primary qualities that an artist must have, but soon the bad fairy came to his bassinet and said, *Child, you will never go any further. Through my power, I now steal from you the qualities which in the end make the artist.*"

As Mira leaned against the wall, she felt an exquisite quivering in her chest, as though something had entered it and was expiring there. But moments later, her skin grew hot and she felt ashamed at the gap between what Albert Wolff was saying and how the painting made her feel. He said that the painting had *some* of the qualities of art, but that there was something missing, the essential thing, the spark that says *more than here.*

"The painting hangs before the spectator with the same qualities of frankness and meaninglessness as the person who is standing before it. One cannot feel dignified by it, or lifted up by it in any way. I am not inspired to think more highly of myself as a man, standing before this painting, than when I stand before a brick wall. I think, *Humans are defeated at the outset—we might as well not even try.* Yet art is supposed to give us the opposite feeling—that human endeavour has wings! A painting should make a person take flight spiritually, but a painting like this one has no wings, so we are given the feeling that wings are not even a thing. The asparagus sits there like a stone in the soul, ridiculing our spiritual pretensions. But spirituality is not a pretension! There is no difference between spirituality and a song, and the song in Manet's heart is the sound of a foghorn. We should feel pity for this desperate and searching boy-painter, who lacks the essential thing, yet doesn't even know it. But to know it, all he would have to do is stand before his painting in any museum, and look right, and look left, and see how the work of the greatest painters makes the soul take flight, then look back at his own painting—vague, rushed, crude, unenchanted, and offering no flight. How can he not see it? A painter with no eyes! Or eyes cut off from his hand! What do humans go to art *for*, but to locate within themselves that inward-turning eye, which breathes significance into all of existence—for what is art but the act of infusing matter with the breath of God? The artist who cannot do this paints irrelevant forms without life. It is obvious why the critics laughed: because they were baffled not to see what they were entitled to see. A person dresses up to go outside, and art must dress up, too. But Manet's paintings are naked, bare—not only in his ridiculous subject matter, but spiritually, as well."

"An artist knows himself to be an artist because of how he relates to his own sincerity," Matty said. "Then would there not have been some uneasiness in Manet while he was painting—some awareness that he lacked the essential thing?" Matty stood there smoking languidly; he was the great, bright hope of the school.

Wolff nodded. "A great artist rests back in the easy chair of his talent, and it's like resting back in the warm hand of God. But Manet's talent does not rest, and he is oblivious to his own stumbling. He is like a dog who walks with three legs, who believes himself no different from a dog who walks with four! He wants the public to do his job—they should simply *feel* enchanted. He asks the public to finish his painting, for he is lazy and incapable. There must be some deep frustration in him as he works, trying to correct what can never be saved. So he paints in a hurried way, not wanting to see what he's made. That's why his canvases are such a mess. There is no compass in his soul, so his vision becomes chaotic. One can sense the envy in his heart, yet he doesn't even know what in other painters to envy! Unable to pull off beauty, he hides behind an ugliness that *he* calls beauty, and his canvases turn out shameful, and so the critics shame him, for he makes us ashamed. Then he continues to make his paintings which have nothing to offer, and turns and blames the critics for their 'crimes.'"

There were so many ways of being hated, and one could be hated by so many people. In the beginning, we were so innocent of this fact—of how much we could be hated, by people we thought would like us, or by people we thought wouldn't care. But there was so much more hate than any of us had the capacity to understand. Hate seemed to spring from the deepest core of our beings. Years later, all you had to do was peep through a peephole and there it was for anyone to see—a whole world of vitriol, entirely without end. It seemed that rage was what we were made of.

And why not? Happiness was not meant to be ours. The love we imagined would never be ours. Work that could occupy our hearts and minds forever—this also was not meant to be ours. We would never make the money we hoped we would make. Nothing would be as we hoped it would be, here in the first draft of existence. People were finally beginning to catch on. Our rage made perfect sense.

At least God had given the sunrise—to those of us who lived on a cliff. At least he had given us a bit of love—if not enough to see us through to the end of our lives. Here in the first draft of existence, we crafted our own second drafts—stories and books and movies and plays—polishing our stones to show God and each other what we wanted the next draft to be, comforting ourselves with our visions. On good days, we acknowledged that God had done pretty well: he had given us life, and had filled in most of the blanks of existence, except for the blank in the heart.

It's true that the world was failing at its one task—of remaining a world. Pieces were breaking off. Seasons had become postmodern. We no longer knew where in the calendar we were by the weather. We once believed that two thousand years ago was long in the past, but then we realized it was actually quite recent—just thirty generations before us. We were still at the stage of perfecting our tools: the bronze age, the iron age, the industrial age, the computer age. But spiritually, there had only ever been one age. Heartbreak was no less heartbreaking. Lust was no less lustful. We remained as proud and hungry and fearful as we had ever been. We could medicate our feelings, a least for a little while, and psychotherapy had taught us to pretend that we were better than we were. Pretending can get you part of the way, but it never gets you far enough.

The ice cubes were melting. The species were dying. The last of the fossil fuels were being burned up. A person collapsing in the street might be collapsing from any one of a hundred things. New things to die of were being added each day.

We were angry all the time. We were envious all the time. We were relieved that we were being looked at by people who were just as angry, and just as envious, as we were. Some people grew nervous that they would be left behind by the times; these people turned their backs on culture and took pleasure in the days passing the way they always had—with the sun rising in the morning, and going down at night. We were curious about the world to come, but were relieved that its problems would not be our own. Some people experienced a delightful sort of rest in becoming very small, very inferior, and very irrelevant, in the face of such chaos and change. Yet in the midst of all this, one could still see, on one's bookshelf, books that were hundreds—even thousands!—of years old, that were relevant today. Yet none of the books which were twenty years old were the least bit relevant anymore.

How a book has to make it through that awkward stage—when it is twenty years too old, yet not quite old enough—before it becomes something natural, an integral part of human civilization, as solid and inevitable as a tree. To become a tree—for a book—is its greatest hope. But how does that happen? And why does it happen to some books, not others? Who is responsible for ushering books forth, and who is merely wearing the clothes of the usher? Who actually leads a book past its awkward and irrelevant years, down through the civilizations?

A cool head and a cold heart are needed to help art prevail. The book-usher has the coldest head and the coolest heart, warmed only by books and words. You can see those who are merely dressed as ushers by their too-hot words. They think that art will warm them, and jump back angry when it bites—

but art is preserved on hearts of ice. It is only those with icebox hearts and icebox hands who have the coldness of soul equal to the task of keeping art fresh for the centuries, preserved in the freezer of their hearts and minds. For art is not made for living bodies—it is made for the cold, eternal soul.

Mira would sit in the lamp store and gaze at one lamp in particular. It had green blobs and red blobs; little polished stones of coloured glass that were held together by a network of iron. The shade was a half-oval, with a beautiful iron stand. It was the most wonderful thing Mira had ever seen. She would sit and wait for the day to turn dark, when she could turn off every other lamp, and stare at her favourite, with its translucent stones illuminated from within. She would spin the shade so gently and its coloured light would fall on the walls and her.

Since the lamp she liked best was the least expensive one, it was possible that one day she might own it, if no one bought it first. Perhaps the fact that it was the least expensive one was the reason she had made it her favourite. There is no point in loving something that is not a bit within reach.

It was the essential humility of the lamp that drew her to it. It had not been made by someone with any sort of insight into how a person might want to appear to others, or who believed that people acquired things to show them off to their friends. It had not been made by someone who imagined that an object fit into a greater system of values, or could place its owner among others with similar taste. It had been made by a humble person who simply thought, *Now I will make my next lamp.*

Whenever Mira came in for her shift, the first thing she did was look to see if the lamp was still there. It always was. She guessed that her boss must know how much she liked it, although she never asked. Probably every employee had their favourite lamp.

One afternoon, they were in the school's tea room, having afternoon tea, when Matty entered and told them that he had just met Annie. Of course they already knew about her—and they were thrilled to learn that she really did exist. Where had he found her? In the park, sitting beneath a tree. He saw her reading and recognized her there. *How could you be sure that it was her?* This was in the early days, before you could look up anyone's picture. He said it was plain to see.

Did you talk to her? Of course he did! As if he would miss the chance! *Well? Did you invite her to Tea?* He said no, like such a thing would be distasteful. But her phone number was written in the back of his book. Well, okay, it wasn't *her* phone number, but the phone number of the bookstore she lived near. They took messages for her there. Mira felt a desperate need to be the one to call, as she was sure—like all of them were—that Annie would change her life. Later, when Mira was even a little bit older, she would have been too shy to meet someone who she thought would change her life. She would have been worried about how she'd appear, or would fear that she'd embarrass herself in some way. But she didn't think of herself as a person back then. She didn't think of herself as someone who another person could see, evaluate, and finally judge. She simply wanted what she wanted, and she didn't think about how her desires would reflect on her.

Matty said, *Come on, let's go call her now.* So that is what they did. They went into the hallway and used the telephone in the wooden box. A woman answered. Matty said he was calling for Annie. The woman said she would take a message. Matty looked at the rest of them, desperate, and whispered, covering the phone, *What's our message?* Mira said, *Tell her to call the registrar and let us know when we can come by.* He asked, *Who's "we"?* But he told the woman that very thing. After he hung up, Matty and Mira argued a bit. He was upset that she had made him say something that sounded stupid and young. *What are you worried about?* Mira asked. *Obviously we're in school.* They tramped down the hall to the registrar's office and went in as a group. Mira explained to the secretary that someone would soon be calling, and could the message please be placed in Matty's box? Each student had a little wooden cubbyhole on the wall outside the office, for mail and private messages and announcements from the school. When they left, Mira said, *You see? It worked out fine.* Matty grimaced. Then they returned to Tea. Two hours later, they went back to his box and found Annie's message waiting for them there. *Come by any night after eight.* What a triumph! They were clearly capable of anything. Everything in their lives was proof of it.

Well, okay, they said, *let's go over now.* They hadn't heard about playing it cool. So at eight o'clock they arrived at the bookshop and opened the glass door in the tiled entry beside the shop, which led up the stairs to Annie's apartment. It was as if they already knew everything about the world—like how their knowledge of Annie included this knowledge of where she lived.

Annie lived in a sprawling apartment above an occult book-store on Harbord Street, back when it was mostly antiquarian bookshops. The smell of the shop filtered up through the vents into her apartment—of incense, strong oils and dusty old crys-tals, dug up deep from the earth, a dark and metallic scent that was like the smell of raw coins, and something of the middle-aged ladies who worked there, with their greying, perfumed flesh. One door led to the occult bookshop and the other led to Annie's apartment, up a dark, narrow corridor of stairs.

Annie's apartment was dusty and smelled of rat shit. It's a smell you don't mistake. Her apartment was just an empty nothing: two bare rooms, one in the front; then, down a long and windowless hallway, a big room in the back. There was a tiny washroom and an awkward kitchen, slotted in between. They wandered around rudely, innocently, curious, as soon as they arrived. The room in the back was emptier, colder. But perhaps at one time it had been pretty and filled with plants, for there was a stack of clay pots in the corner, which Annie hadn't bothered to throw out. Both rooms had plenty of win-dows, but the first time they went over, it was evening, and the windows just reflected back their sorry faces, while on the out-side was the watery night. In the kitchen was an old stove which gave off the smell of leaking gas, but those were the days when everything smelled bad. All of their apartments stank. But each one stank differently, and how one's apartment smelled was a source of some personal pride, like their apartment was their own armpit: one felt a bit attracted to the smell, and defensive on its behalf. The front room had a low wood coffee table and a few sagging chairs that were pushed up against the walls, clearly dragged in from the street.

Mira suddenly felt embarrassed to be there with her classmates. She wanted to distinguish herself; for Annie to know that she was the best one, the one who Annie should like best. Matty had pretentiously doffed his cap to Annie as soon as they entered. They finally settled into the front room, on cushions on the floor. Annie returned from the kitchen with a large and overflowing sea-shaped ashtray, which she placed in the middle of the table, and they all pulled out their cigarettes. Mira followed Annie's gaze, and wondered if Annie wanted to fuck Matty—Matty who smelled of basements, yet was appealing nonetheless.

All around them were floating all sorts of ghosts and spirits that they had no time for. In the houses they rented were the ghosts and leftover everythings of the people who had lived and died there, and the people who had died before those people lived, on the land and in it, and just everything forming the carbon of everything that was the stage and amphitheatre of their entire lives, which they never once considered.

They wouldn't have known how to talk about it, if they had thought about it, but they didn't think about it, or that whatever was happening to them was happening on a graveyard. And how were they to know that the sweetest one of them all would die from some unthinkable disease, twenty years on, just a few blocks from where their parties had been, a disease which came on strong and fast, then locked her in so that none of them knew if she could hear what they were saying. *Could* she hear them, or was her brain mush? She had been like Mira; she didn't play the girl games. Then one day, before it made any sense, she was dead.

~

The only way they could live with their sense of total importance which was the core of everything they experienced was because the messages from the outside world were so, so limited. They came through the daily newspapers, if at all. They didn't even read the papers. They never saw a video of how another girl fixed her hair. They didn't even know that other girls fixed their hair. Everything, other lives, and the thoughts of people who were not themselves, were all so equally far away. All that touched them was each other, and the books they read, and the music. Did any other kids exist? They certainly didn't think so.

Can we say that friendships were different then? That they were like lamps, alone with you in your total privacy? One knew no more than a dozen or two dozen people, and you never knew when you would see them again. There was always the chance, after you parted, that it was for the last time. After a party, it was always possible that you would never see their faces ever again. It wasn't even something you thought about. Everyone had their own little life, which touched the lives of other people only at parties. Between the parties, there was no interaction with most.

There was nothing show-offy about friendships then. Your friends were simply who was around. It didn't occur to anyone that it could be another way. If you liked your friends, that was okay. If you didn't like your friends, that was okay, too. We were fine with living our mediocre lives. It didn't occur to anyone that we could have great ones. That was for people far away. Our lack of awareness of the scope of the world kept us from any great falseness. It was enough to know just four or five people, and to have slept with two or three of them. Was there anything else to be ambitious for? Just an imagined immortality—a sense of one's own greatness, which could in no way be tested.

It wasn't that long ago, is the funny thing. We are, for the most part, all of us still alive. Yet none of us keep in touch with the other ones. We only keep in touch with the friends we have made since the friendship revolution, which made being in touch of primary importance. The friends we knew from way back when—we felt content to let them slip away; to continue the traditions of the old world into now.

One day, while at work, Mira's boss pulled on his coat, saying he needed to run a bit of an errand, and that he would be back in twenty minutes. As soon as he left, Mira took her favourite lamp and hurried with it to the back of the shop and hid it near the fire door, out in the alley, among the folded cardboard boxes and sagging bags of trash.

Hours later, after closing, Mira went out the front door and around to the back, where she found the lamp and carried it carefully down many streets, concealed beneath her coat. She carried the lamp like it was the fattest cat, clasped to her chest and held tightly. She took it to her room and put it on her desk. She leaned down to plug it in, then sat up again and looked at it. There it was: her lamp.

~

Mira didn't think that having the lamp would make her more valuable, or turn her into an impressive sort of person. She didn't think anyone would admire her for having the lamp. She didn't think it would give her magical powers. It was just the desire to have something so special, so glowing, and entirely her own. It had been a simple and pure thing, her wanting it. Later, acquiring things would become more complicated, and would leave her dissatisfied, confused, and wanting even more. But having the lamp didn't lead her to wanting more lamps. It led only to the pleasure of having this lamp.

She got up and turned off the overhead light, then returned to sit before it. The red and green stones shed its light upon her dark face and the white walls. And she loved her meagre little existence, which was entirely her own.

They had planned the whole thing themselves, the dinner. They were going to invite everyone, all the best people they knew. Mira had moved out of her first apartment, and was now living in a house with Matty and two classmates. She told them that she was hoping to invite Annie, announcing it as though she would be asking the queen. They had run into her a few more times since they had all sat on the floor of her apartment that night. They hoped she would say yes.

~

That night, fifteen of them sat around a few makeshift tables, eating the peanut soup which had been prepared by their skinny vegan roommate, who lived in the attic upstairs, and who collected anarchist notebooks and tarnished Japanese swords.

None of them had hosted a dinner before, and Annie was someone Mira truly admired. Then why did she invite her to their squalid home? Because until Annie appeared at their front door, Mira had no awareness of how her life would appear to Annie. Mira had invited her, bursting with pride, thinking that she would see Mira's life the same way Mira did—as a coolly admirable existence. But as soon as Annie entered the vestibule, Mira knew that inviting her had been a mistake. Walking through the hallway, Mira saw Annie glance at the painting that Matty had found in the street. He had hung the landscape in the hallway and had adorned it with painted dicks in all the most hilarious places. Mira now saw, from Annie's glance, that there was nothing fantastic about it at all. What Matty had done was juvenile and dumb! So was their life, so was their party, so was the soup, and so were their drunk and too-young friends, none of who knew how to behave at what they had loftily called a *dinner party*.

Was Annie wrong to find the food disgusting and everyone there contemptible? Was she wrong to be put off when they all got so rowdily drunk within the first two hours, and began insulting the vegan and his peanut soup, and threw his bread all over the room? Mira watched Annie anxiously, at the way she sat, her posture erect, her chair pushed back from the rest. Annie was not drunk, she was not smiling, and Mira couldn't put a stop to any of it.

Annie didn't stay long at the party.

Over the next few weeks, any time Mira and Annie ran into each other, something widened inside of them. Something was opening in Mira's chest, a portal to Annie and her open chest, which was widening in the direction of Mira. This widening was something that Mira had never felt before, or even known could be. It was like a vagina was stretching for a very large cock, but it was in her chest that this stretching was happening, in the part of her that usually kept love out, that firmly preserved her insides. This was how she normally lived—with that part of her sealed shut. But now it was opening almost too wide, and a similar thing was happening in Annie.

~

What of the strength of our connections with certain people, and the weakness of our connections with certain other ones? Seeing Annie for the first time, something in Mira recognized her. It was like their relationship already existed. It wasn't this way with most other people. It was Annie's apparent pre-existence, which seemed impossible to explain, which distinguished her from the rest. And it was strange for Mira to think that, for other people, Annie was just someone passing on the street, that she was nothing at all.

With a few people in one's life, too much happens emotionally—more than even makes sense to happen, given how little has actually occurred. Such people are deeply igniting in a way that others are not. This igniting always happens in the very first instant and it never goes away. No stupidities can destroy the igniting, so even if those two people never meet again, a connection always remains. Mira felt this way about Annie. It wasn't that Mira had met her in some previous life. It was that she was meeting her *in this one*—and isn't that rare! Why is it so hard to meet *in this life*?

But the deeper question was: What was one supposed to do with such people? Fuck them, love them, or leave them alone? Yet they seemed to call out to be acted upon. Mira could feel it. But this had the potential of making her a nuisance in their life. What was she supposed to do about the fact that she was experiencing a widening towards Annie? Yet to do something in response to this feeling could easily be embarrassing, because Mira didn't know if Annie felt called to be in *Mira's* life. Surely not everyone Mira felt called towards could believe their life was about a meeting with *her*.

～

On such occasions, it is often the gods who are to blame. They slip into a person like an amoeba, and from within one person, they watch another one—the one they have chosen to watch.

So from within Annie, the gods were watching Mira, and from within Mira, the gods were watching Annie. It doesn't always happen mutually this way, but in their case it did—the gods just taking notes on humans, to make us better in the next draft of the world. Mira, who knew nothing of this, wondered what the intensity meant: Why *Annie* of all people on this earth? Why could she not stop thinking about *Annie*?

Every time they glanced at each other, or thought of each other a little bit, their chests widened more. They noticed hidden things about the other one, without even meaning to. All this seemed to be happening of its own accord, this laying down of a bridge on which things between them could pass; not necessarily sexual things, or even intimate things, but things as yet unknown. A road was being laid, though nothing was yet travelling on that road. Some workers were doing it—it was the gods—and it was happening far too quickly! They always worked so fast—so much faster than humans could ever understand. Mira felt nervous and confused: nothing of significance had even happened in the few times they had seen each other to account for such a solid road. The experience was painful, like her rib cage was being pried apart, so that worker hands could get at her heart. Then she could no longer deny the fact of this road that was being laid between them, straight into the deepest corner of Mira's chest, normally shuttered, now flung open wide; and if neither was ready to walk on the road quite yet, it was hard to believe they wouldn't soon be walking on it.

Annie had grown up in an orphanage in a faraway American city, so Mira and her friends thought she was special—to have come from a country so marvellously bleak, and to have never met her parents. She told them stories about what the orphans had got up to, with their singing and their dancing, their mischief and their tears; their leaning up against an open window and looking out over their great and sparkling city, wondering if their parents were out there; if they remembered the child they gave up, and if they were rich or pretty or kind.

Being an orphan made her better than they were, all of them agreed. America made her better, too. She had eaten sweets they had only heard about—*Mikes and Ikes. What were those?* What was it like not to know where you came from, or why your parents had given you up?

They could not imagine what her life had been. They longed to be like Annie—so independent, so free. There was something romantic about having grown up without parents, but the idea also scared them. A mother and father was all that they knew, even if they weren't living with them now. Even if they never called them on the phone, there would always be an umbrella over them, if it rained. They could get wet if they wanted to, but if they wanted to stay dry, their parents would come. They didn't know that this was where their courage derived from, or that their imagined striking out was no more bold than an evening stroll down a well-lit street. They could go home if they wanted to. They had parents who loved them. Mira had a father who loved her so much, nearly to the exclusion of everyone else. While Annie had no one, she was completely alone. That was why they were drawn to her. Mira and her friends admired her deeply. She was who they were pretending to be.

Perhaps Mira shouldn't have left home so young, for something changed upon her moving out. It meant leaving behind the traditional and warm values she had known—for what? A difficult life on the knife-edge of feelings, since that's what being an art critic meant: an existence hard up against the sharp knife-edge of life.

~

When Mira thought about home, her main thought was about her father, and about how he wanted her near. He encouraged her to go out in the world, but he would have rather she stayed at home with him. She always felt his presence, calling her to return, and she could never separate any of her actions from the pleasure or the pain she feared it would cause him—her total suspicion of which way it would go.

In her childhood, everything between them had been golden and green: he was always pointing out the beauty of the world to her, its greatness and its mystery, and his attention had made her feel cherished and loved.

One sunny afternoon, when Mira and her father were

standing in the garden, he promised that one day he would buy her all sorts of mysterious, rare and marvellous things, including *pure colour*—not something that was coloured, but colour itself! Colour itself came in hard little circular discs, and was shiny like a polished stone or polished jewel, but with its colour deep inside it. It showed its colour on the outside, for its outside was what it was all the way through. But unlike a gemstone, it didn't emanate colour. Its colour sat there, turned inwards. Pure colour was introverted, like a shy little animal. Mira had never seen pure colour before, but she guessed there was probably lots that her father knew about, and could show her, and give her, besides these discs.

~

As Mira got older, it became harder to love him in the proper dimensions, or even to know what those were; any interest she developed in another person felt like it was taking something from him, since he had no one to love but Mira. It was generally a pleasure to be with him, but something always interfered. It was the heat of his fur, which followed her everywhere—clinging and itchy; but also comforting, home.

So Mira craved to live a cold ice bath of a life, once she was out in the world, without him. It had been hard to be held so closely by the most bearish bear, and anyone who approached her with the same total love immediately made Mira feel scared. She was more drawn to the fish, who divided their attention democratically among people. So the overheated Mira went looking for a freezer. She wanted a love that would cool her down, to the temperature of the living. She longed to be held by the coldest hands. If she was loved in a way that warmed her up, she feared she would be too hot to handle art, to help pass it down through the centuries.

Mira hadn't meant to kiss Annie on the back of the neck, so sensually, the first time they were alone together, outside. They were standing in the doorway of the bookshop, up near the street. Then Mira was genuinely overtaken. She started kissing Annie on her neck, then heard Annie's breath grow fainter, then she continued for a bit longer, then stopped. It was the first time in her life that she had been so overcome. It was lust, but it was also a sudden kind of love. She had only meant to push aside a lock of Annie's hair, and plant a little kiss behind it. Mira was the unassuming sort of person who, in those days, could get away with such a thing—but when she planted her lips, the deep smell of Annie kept her there, close up against the heat of her neck. So she kissed her a bit longer, kissing her neck gently with the softest lips, and there was more silence in the air around Mira as she did this than there had ever been before. The silence was a silence in her heart, as well.

There was something about Annie, some power she had, that Mira didn't recognize until she was kissing her. Then she understood that she was under some spell—and she thought she knew why men down through the ages had often feared women, feeling them to possess some otherworldly power that had to be reined in. Mira was suddenly filled with all the things she could do with Annie, all the things she would have loved to do, letting herself be led with no thought at all—with the same blankness in her mind that she felt as she kissed her—and she knew that she could keep going with even deeper regions of her body and heart. She saw a future unfurling between them, even as she tried to resist it, but she had never before seen a future so convincingly unfurl.

~

In the weeks that followed, Annie didn't mention what happened, and as Mira was young and inclined to shame, they never spoke of it again.

Feces, worms, piss, trouble. This is where we are now. Our dressing up has led us nowhere; our manners have led us nowhere. Being in love was just a fantasy of a world that was not entirely piss and dust. But what a fantasy Annie's face provoked! In some books, you are supposed to stay away from such a woman, but in other books, she is the one you are supposed to love. In life, there are no sure signs of whether a woman is the one you are supposed to stay away from, or the one you're supposed to love.

A person can waste their whole life, without even meaning to, all because another person has a really great face. Did God think of this when he was making the world? Why didn't he give everyone the exact same face? Perhaps it will be like that in the next draft of the world, and people living in that time might not even imagine that there was ever a draft in which everyone had a different face. Although the thought might disgust them, it will not lead them to thinking about how much time our various faces wasted. They will not think about how some faces ruined the lives of people with less beautiful faces, or how having a beautiful face could ruin the life of the person who had one.

But doesn't it all work out in the end, no matter which face you got? Yes, people with ugly faces can lead beautiful lives, and people with beautiful faces can lead ugly ones, and a beautiful face can draw you right down deep into the world's greatest ugliness. But in the next draft of existence, they will not understand this; how one person's beautiful face could pull another person deep into their greatest sorrow.

Some months later, Annie put a photograph of herself, which she had developed in a darkroom downtown, into a book she had borrowed from Mira, that she was now returning. Mira didn't find the photo until many years later, opening the book to discover this surprising proof of Annie's affection. Or perhaps Annie had simply forgotten it there? Maybe she had been using it as a bookmark? But no, for when she turned over the picture, she saw, in Annie's awkward handwriting, the words *For Mira*.

Why didn't Annie, in the weeks after she returned the book, say to Mira, *I hope you found my picture*? Because Annie would never have said such a thing. She had too much pride and was too filled with despair to ever say to anyone, *Did you find my picture?* Mira was the unthinking sort of person who could have said to anybody, *Did you find my picture?* but Annie was too cool and too utterly hurt to ever utter those words.

Being an orphan was Annie's first experience of life, so it is possible that she felt doomed to repeat the experience—of being there, but overlooked. The days of the present often mimic the past, like a duckling following its mother—and who has ever been able to persuade the babyish present *not* to follow the mother duck of the past? So instead of giving Mira the photo, she left it where it wouldn't be seen.

More time passed, months went on, and there was a sort of slackening, like a season was coming undone. You could smell the rotting end of it. How at the end of summer you can already smell the autumn, breezing down from the leaves. And how at the end of autumn you can smell the winter, in the frost sharpening the ground.

Matty was the first one to feel it. A wide-hipped woman caught his eye, who was unlike the rest of them in every way, and he went off and married her, leaving the rest of them there.

They soon began drinking in different cafés, exchanged a few letters, then stopped. For they had all taken it as a sign—that all it took was for Matty to fall in love for their whole world to slacken and fall apart.

So that is what it was, looking backwards. Mira would have needed a new thermos to put it all in, since the one she had couldn't keep her memories warm enough.

As the past cooled, it changed states. It had once been a solid, then it became a gas. Or it had been a gas first, then it became a liquid, and she was left holding the muck of it in her hands. And she thought, *All that time, all that stupid time, I should have been with my father.*

TWO

She doesn't know how to think about her father's death, or even if she should, or how to explain the great joy and calm that settled in her the moment the life left his body, and she felt his spirit enter her, and fill her up with joy and light. There was a moment when there was nothing, no life in him left, then the spirit that had been in her father entered her. It came in through her chest and she felt it there in her entire body— near the top of her skull, down in her toes, swirling wonderfully inside her, and the peace she knew after it settled inside her was the cleanest feeling of love; a brightness that finally compelled her to sit up, having felt it swirling long enough that now it seemed time to share it, to go downstairs and hug her uncle, and tell him, *Dad is dead*, and to try and hug him close enough that maybe he could feel it, too; her father's love that was streaming through her. So complete was the feeling of peace and joy, and relief for her father that it was all done, the difficult endeavour that had been his life, and the carrying of all that was heavy—it was over, and out of the deflation of his body came the purest joy. Then, maybe twenty minutes later, such a deep chill came over her, and her teeth started chattering, and they would not stop clacking together, and her arms were freezing up, and her entire body was freezing and chattering, so that she returned back upstairs to her father's body and sat beside him in his bed, and pulled the covers up, not even looking at him, but trying to warm her body there. Had his spirit left her? Or was the chattering because of what had happened, and his spirit remained inside her, but such an event would naturally be followed by the deepest chills? But there was no asking anyone on earth, for we haven't been created to know it.

She lay beside him, holding him, her arm over his chest, her body pressed up against the side of his now-still and lifeless body, which had been breathing mere moments before, and she knew that her brain was a small and useless, earth-bound thing that would never understand, and that she would never be able to properly reconstruct what she had just experienced.

Later, walking in the garden out behind his house, another hour deep into the middle of the night, she knew that the universe had ejaculated his spirit into her—and was it still in her? What if, when she was shivering and chilled and her teeth were chattering, half an hour after it happened, it was because his spirit had suddenly left her? She will never know, and there is no authority on earth who can say what happened that night. It was happening on the spiritual plane—it was not a physical, psychological, or emotional phenomenon, so she will never understand.

~

When the doctor came later that night to proclaim him dead, and took her hand and said, *Sorry for your loss*, standing there with this new, joyful and loving spirit inside of her, she almost laughed at this strange word he was using, *loss*.

When Mira thinks about her father's death, or the few days of his dying, certain elements are returned to her: his bedroom, the smell of his body from under the sheets as he moved his legs and the air escaped, and she smelled a sort of shit she had never before smelled, intensely pungent, a shit that was also tar. She remembers the darkness of his room, a room which she had known: the bookshelves, the desk beside the bed, and the chair beside the bed that she sometimes sat in that week. How her uncle had put up cardboard-backed prints of paintings, leaning them against the windows to block out the light, and a green towel which he had taped up. From where did he get the tape? She remembers the pink towel on the floor by her father's bed, where he placed his feet, and the bathroom rug she had brought and eventually put in place of the towel; it was fluffier, warmer, and it didn't slip. Her uncle thought he would not appreciate the change, but he did. No, the towel on the floor wasn't pink. It was green. Colours matter. Colours can be hard to remember.

There was the smell of the beeswax candle that she ordered online, which burned the entire time on the little white-and-black-flecked plate. There was the deep yellow of the candle. There was the pink glass of the scented lamp which she had brought from home with its scent of fresh linen, which became too strong to keep burning. Those scents were the scent of the room, mixed with the smell of her father dying, and the difficult sound of his breathing, which she missed each time she left the room. It was like the sound of the sea, or a boat on the sea; aching, creaking, rhythmic, hard. It was difficult for him to breathe, but she loved the sound, and the sound also pained her and put her in a trance. Whenever she went downstairs, if she was gone for too long, she longed for it. It was the sound of him alive, and the very last sounds he made. Though the last sound he made was no sound at all—the sound of the breath that did not come.

~

The more she thinks about the sort of maroonish light in his room those nights, and the light of the candle flickering, she knows that the colour of that room is how they all felt, and that colour is not just a representation of the world, but of the feelings in a room, and the meaningfulness of a room in time, because in that colour, her father died. She had never seen that colour before. It was the colour of a father dying.

In the days before her father died, she felt all her memories of him disappearing; everything he ever said was gone. She thought, *Oh, life is so stupid, it all means nothing, nothing we do ever lasts, what is the point of it all?*

On those final days, with him mostly unconscious, and sometimes a bit conscious, and sometimes squeezing her hand, she felt how precious it was to be in a room with him, and she wished she had done it more, just gone over to his house with no expectation of talking, just sitting in a room. She suddenly understood how much he had needed that, and now she understood its value, and how lonely it would have been for him not to have had it enough, and now it was all she wanted too, and they would never have it again.

Control your mind, she told herself sternly and seriously through his final hours and days. She knew his death was sending her into the future, and she wanted it to be a bearable one. *Control your mind*, she said to herself, so she wouldn't go down the deepest path of recrimination and despair. What were the words that came into her mind, as she lay with him in the darkness of his final days? *For there is nothing either good or bad, but thinking makes it so.*

It seemed to her the week her father was dying that nothing mattered but art and literature. That while people passed away, the soul of a great artist would stay; that what they made would never die, so they were the ones we could hold close forever. Art would never leave us like a father dying. In a way, it would always remain. Artists manifested themselves in art, not the world, so humans could encounter them there, forever. People could return to books at any time and find them right there, those burning souls, their words as bright as the day they were written. How Mira loved artists! How she loved books, as she lay in bed with her dying father. She saw how great art was, as she lay in his bed, and how faithful; how faithful a book was, and how strong, a place you could be safe, apart from the world, held inside a world that would never grow weak, and which could pass through wars, massacres and floods—could pass through all of human history, and the integrity of its soul would stay strong. A writer could suspend their soul in language, making the souls of writers like droplets of oil, suspended in the sea of life. You couldn't see the water, but you could see the drops, clear little circles, buoyant and complete. To be in a world in which the writers she loved had once lived and written beautifully—that meant there was something real to find here. Art had mattered to her most of all, but her father mattered, also, yet now she saw why she hadn't been the daughter he'd wanted her to be; because art had meant more to her than any human being, it meant more to her than her father did. Her love for her father was great, but her love for books was greater. Had he known this? He once called her selfish. She knew that she had loved her father more than many other people loved theirs. But there was something she loved above her father. This was something they had never seen or could even understand. She didn't even see it until he lay there, dying. Then, in bed with him, her arm across his rising chest, rising and falling those remaining days, and staring at his bookshelf, at all six volumes of Churchill's memoirs, she realized this bottom truth about the nature of her love, and that there was no bottom below this bottom.

His spirit was sly as a fox, the way it snuck into her—the way it stealthily, like a fox, moved into her. She can still feel it there, sometimes, sneaking about. It is a great joy to have his spirit inside her, like the brightest and youngest fox! It rests when it wants to, it moves when it wants to, it lives out its days, in her. So many gifts her father gave her, so she should not be surprised they continued to be given, even in the moment of his dying. His whole life had been a giving to her of his life, and even in death he was giving; like in a fable when a poor man pulls a handful of jewels, emeralds and sapphires from an empty linen sack. So it was as if pulled from his dead body—that empty sack—were the brightest and most shimmering stars, which was his entire spirit.

She had held him when he died, and the heat that filled her was his spirit entering, which spread through the interior of her innermost darkness with an exploding and infinite light.

But she doesn't know the rules of the spirit world, so she will never be able to explain.

In the weeks that followed her father's dying, her mind returned and returned her to it, but she could no more re-create what happened than she could physically return to the past. It was impossible to properly recall it, meaning that she would only know if his spirit had entered her if she had been changed.

But how does she know if she has been changed, or if she just so much wants to be changed that since it happened, she has been pretending?

Yet now she feels exactly how she always wanted to feel, like all her deficiencies have been filled up, all her sorry spaces, and all her spiritual empties. Her sufferings, her stupidities, her utter inabilities, which no instructions or reminders to herself and no aging or learning could ever correct—her father's spirit filled up these empty spaces like water filling up a half-empty cup, or an entire table of half-empty cups. Why? It was perhaps one of two things: the last gift her father, in his generosity, gave her, or else this is what the universe always intended to happen, to complete and make whole the life within her with the addition of her father's spirit, bearing all the gifts and wisdom that her own self was lacking.

The gifts of patience, perspective and detachment.

The gifts of silence, irrelevance and joy.

The day or second day after he died, she saw falling from the sky the first sprinklings of snow. She had never felt a greater quiet in her mind or soul. She cared nothing for the world's busy activity. She felt in competition with no one.

Then there was too much to feel, being outside; the cold breath of the universe, breathing on her face and neck. She used to prefer to be inside, but now with her father gone, she prefers to be outside because she needs the company. She needs the breath of the universe, for she will never feel the breath of her father again. Yet outside she can feel the breath of everything, and the breath of the whole world is the breath of her father—if there is even such a thing as a father.

She doubts it. She thinks it must have been an illusion, that she was only told, *This is your father.* For now that her father is gone, they were obviously only words; for if now she can exist without a father, she could always have existed without a father—because she is not his child, just matter infused with spirit, which makes her live. If she can exist without her father, perhaps she could always have existed without him; she didn't need a father and she didn't need a mother in order to be alive. All that was needed was for spirit to blow into her flesh. So our relation to others is not what we think. It is our relation to spirit that makes us alive. The clouds don't have a father, yet they still live. The trees don't have a mother or father, yet they live as much as we do.

Life rushed at her after her father died, as if to remind her that there can be no less life, that there can be no deprivation of life, that life is an endless and eternal living, even if your father is dead.

At times, but not when she is smoking, she can still feel his spirit inside her, twinkling like the brightest stars in her chest. And she can feel what stills or mutes them. Nothing makes them dance like her own aloneness. In her utter privacy, they dance for joy.

~

If the spirit of a father can move into a daughter, this must be happening all over the world, spirits entering other bodies, when a person dies. So there is always the possibility for a second draft in a human life, for life is always revolving, exiting a dying thing and mixing with the living. There is always the chance to live newly, to be born into a second life, for the spirit and you.

Who will her spirit explode into when she dies—if anyone? Yet she doesn't even care if it's not anyone. When the spirit of her father came into her, it paused a moment in the air between them where it was purified, and then what entered her was the purest love and elation. This is what the universe ejaculated into the deepest cells of her, or into what is deeper than cells.

Now walking outside, her hands quake, and her heart quivers and quakes, and there is a quivering and quaking in her chest and heart, from the whole world breathing on her, and she had never known that it was all so alive. She never knew that through her entire life she was walking in the spirit of everything, and that the whole world—trees and breezes and leaves and air—was just as alive as her father had been. Because she had been so aware of the life of her father, she had not been enough aware of how alive the rest of it was. She had been too much looking at him. All her life, breezes were blowing on her cheeks, but this was something she did not notice. She had not understood that the spirit that animated the body of her father animated the body of everything. Trees and the sky were not a backdrop to life, but they were equally life. She thought, *I am the daughter of everything*, but then she thought, *No, I am not the daughter of anything. There are no daughters anywhere on earth.*

After his spirit went into her, certain things seemed horrible, and like abominations: cigarettes, that vial of marijuana oil, alcohol less than cigarettes, but alcohol felt like an abomination, too. So many things felt horrible to her, an offense to the new spirit inside her, and the drugs had the effect of tamping it down. But she did begin drinking coffee and reading the news, and smoking a cigarette now and then, even though she felt how doing these things was tamping the spirit down.

In those early dreams, in which her father returned from the dead, she felt scared for him, and for herself, too. She also felt upset. In the world of those early dreams, she understood that the best and only good thing about death was that it was final. That there could be no negotiating with death was its one mercy, its only relief.

In those early dreams, her father came back from the dead to show her that he had figured out how to return; a prideful demonstration, and more proof of the stupidity of other people, that they didn't even try to return after they'd died. They followed the conventions—in death as in life—while he, who had always defied convention, had come back to life to show her that it was just social norms that kept other people in their graves.

This really scared her. *Didn't he know he had been cremated?* Maybe she didn't understand what cremation was.

She didn't know what to do with him in these dreams. She sensed that he was making a mistake, and feared that his second death would be worse than his first. She knew it was her responsibility to tell him he was dead, but would he believe her? Would he get mad? Her father, who refused to act like an adult in life—who had insisted his whole life that he was still a child—could never be told to act dead. He would have been appalled at her conventionality; that she wanted him to be like other humans, and die.

In the first draft of their lives together, there had always been a push and pull between them, always a closeness and a desire to be rid of that closeness, neither of them being able to fix their uncomfortable nearness and farness, or to understand what distance was best. Then they were in one body, hers. Or they had been, for an instant. She had felt his spirit ejaculate into her, like it was the entire universe coming into her body, then spreading all the way through her, the way cum feels spreading inside, that warm and tangy feeling. But this feeling was even warmer, and even more spreading all the way through her, and the peace after an orgasm was nothing compared to the peace that fell over her after his death. And the peace that fell over his body was just as complete. There is no peace as complete as to die. It is the end of your story and the end of you. For the living, their stories are still going on. There is strife until death, and there are always problems between people, and even when there are no problems, problems are still there. Being alive is a problem that cannot be solved with living. The self is ever stirred like the leaves in the trees. The leaves quiver and quake, just like we do. A person cannot stop their quivering and quaking, which is the essence of a human life. But no danger comes to the one who is dead. Their problems with everyone are through.

She has given herself no time to determine if the spirit of her father is still inside her, but—*Oh there! She can feel it! Rising in her chest!* It was not gone, but sleeping, dormant, waiting to be called! It does not know its way around her yet. It does not know where in her body it wants to be. She will have to help it—to stop her smoking and look into her chest, where this new spirit grows, rising. When it senses that she is looking for it, it expresses a surge of joy just to be seen—the same way her father expressed joy when she went to see him or called. He was always so happy just to see her. In the exact same way, his spirit is happy to be near. Perhaps her father wanted her so close simply because the spirit inside of him did, for inside of her lived his spirit's kin—but in his life they were held apart in two separate bodies. Then they were, at last, reconciled.

Was there something wrong with her father's spirit going into her after he died? More of what had oppressed her in her living? The life in him had always wanted to join her, and in his death, it finally did. For many years, his desire to be so close had been a bit of a problem, but in death it had become the most beautiful thing. In life, he had given her his entire life, but this had been a problem. In death, he had given her what remained of his life, and this was the most beautiful thing.

Perhaps we can only give in total beauty and simplicity in the moment of our dying, because that is the only giving that demands no return. Once you are dead, you can no longer accept a return, but in life there is always the hope of being given in return. Her father had wanted to give to her in life the same way he had given to her in death, so completely unselfishly. And he had, he had. And he hadn't, he hadn't.

Perhaps this is why Mira doesn't like loving people. Perhaps this is why she doesn't like being loved. Just because it's love, does that mean you have to like it? Do you have to want it forever, simply because it's love? Maybe Mira has no heart. Maybe a heart comes and goes. Maybe her heart is protecting her against pain. Perhaps it will start working later on. Perhaps her heart got tired long ago, and collapsed and was left by the side of the road. Maybe one day it will start to feel again. Maybe it has run out of feelings. Anything can run out of anything. A thought can run out of words.

The last thing that's needed is to judge your own heart, but then that's the first thing you go and do. A heart rushes to judge itself. A heart should have better things to do. A heart doesn't.

The day after her father died, Mira saw that she could abandon her whole life, walk away from it, and it wouldn't matter. He had abandoned his life, so she could abandon hers, too. She understood, watching her father die, that there was no reason to be afraid of anything. She could no longer be afraid of living or dying. And her father, who had actually loved his life, told her on his deathbed, *None of this matters.*

Did he work for his own death? He seemed to slip into it, like slipping into a pool of water, slowly but with determination, a knowledge that this was right. It was where he wanted to go, at a certain point, and so he went there, slipped right into it until he was completely submerged and could no longer rise to the surface. She knew that one day death would find her, the same way it had found him—but that this was nothing to fear, or to feel too sad about, for there would always be something vaster that would hold you in its arms, something vaster even than a loving daughter. You would be held in the universe's arms, but you would also *be* its arms. Was she supposed to fear becoming the blood and the electrical impulses in the arms of the entire universe?

She was finally at peace in his bed, holding him. Which she would never have done if he was not dying—just lying in the same bed as him, warming him in her arms. All the complications of modern psychology had prevented her from ever doing that, or from even thinking she might have wanted to. Her lonely father, who had no woman besides Mira.

Then she missed being beside him, as he lay there, dying. To hear him breathe with difficulty, to hold his thin and shiny hand. As she lay in bed with him, in those final days, she made herself feel what it was like to be near her father while he was still living, because she knew it was the end of her feeling it forever.

She wanted to remain there beside him for weeks and months. In those days, she abandoned all other people, and all the things that had mattered to her. She believed they never would matter again.

All she was called to do was to lie there beside him, and it was the most important thing. She was just a body beside a body. During his life, doing this hadn't felt like an important thing. How had she missed the truth?

Then the next day comes, and it implies a day after that. Yet her life has come to feel like just one day, a day in which she both has a father and doesn't have one. There is no one to call, although a hundred times a day she thinks, *I really should call him.* There is no one to visit, no one to do anything for.

To be a daughter is to be leaning, half. To no longer be a daughter is to be a whole thing, an orb. From inside her orb, she can see other people more clearly than before. They seem more tender to her now. It is not because she understands that they will die, but because she now has the time and ability to see them, which she did not before, when she was a daughter, and had a father, and was looking out from within their orb. Other people were always in the background of her father. They weren't as important as he was. They didn't need her as much as he did. Now that she is without him, she sees other people as if for the first time. They are not merely *not her father*—as she wasn't even aware they were then.

She passed weeks in bed, hours and hours, just playing the jewel game on her phone. The game was easy and beautiful, and she felt she was very good at it. Every time she played, she would think, *After this game, you will put down your phone and do something else*, but she never put down her phone, and she never did something else. She continued to play the jewel game. She thought, *It's okay, don't worry, you won't play the jewel game forever*. But what if she *did* play the jewel game forever?

She thought about her entire life as she arranged jewels upon jewels. She thought about her life very slowly. She felt her brain get slow, clear and focussed. Organizing jewels took care of the nervous part of her brain, and replaced it with the pleasant sensation of having done a good job cleaning jewels. She felt like she was creating order in the universe as the jewels disappeared. As she was clearing away jewels, she wondered, *Isn't it time yet to become part of the world?*

What world? After all, the world was also right where she was living. Her bed was as much the world as anything outside it. The world included her phone, her bed, these jewels. The world included her doing this. How could she ever become *more* a part of it? So she cleaned away the jewels, assured there was nowhere she had to go.

One afternoon, she stopped her crying and answered the phone and sat up and talked to her uncle for half an hour. Her roommate's large dog lay sleeping on the couch, where Mira had just been lying on him. When she hung up the phone, she lay back down on the dog, resting her cheek against his back, and was surprised to find his fur all wet from her tears.

She doesn't know why she spent so much of her life thinking about such trivial things, or looking at websites, when just outside her window there was a sky that was not trivial. Had it been wrong of her not to understand that the sky was more valuable than a website? People once valued the sky, but only because they had nothing better—because they didn't have websites. It was hard to tell which was right: either the sky was more valuable than a website, or a website was more valuable than the sky. If she gathered together the amount of time she spent looking at websites, and the amount of time she spent looking at the sky, then her life was clearly answering which was the more valuable, for her.

She and her father will never sit and look at a movie screen together, and the thought of never going to a movie with him again makes her miss him so unbearably, as though that was all they did, as though that was their favourite thing they did together. Was it? Maybe it was.

She didn't realize it at the time, but now it's clear, it *was* their favourite thing. Why didn't they do it more often? Probably there wasn't always a good movie playing. Probably she was "busy."

She had thought that when someone died, it would be like they went into a different room. She had not known that life itself transformed into a different room, and trapped you in it without them.

She wanted her father to know how bad she was feeling. She didn't want to get over the pain. She didn't have the energy to make the best of it. She didn't see what purpose it would serve to make the best of something in a world that felt stripped of any arrows, any direction, any sense. Who would she be making the best of it for? *Herself?* She didn't care about herself. Her father, who wasn't there? The living? It was the dead who needed our love, the dead who she wanted to be loyal to, the dead who needed us most. The living could take care of themselves, going to the grocery store in all that sunshine. It was the dead who needed to be held on to, so they would not slip away. Who would save the dead from oblivion, if not we, the living? She would have to hold on to her father forever so he would not slip away.

That winter, walking through her neighbourhood, she saw the little red, green, white, blue, purple and yellow Christmas lights, which dotted the porches and were strung across the trees in the front yards of most of her neighbours. They shimmered like the most beautiful stars, just giving off their humble light, their cords curled and mangled, their plastic—obvious— but they shimmered like the souls of a million long-dead people. That humans felt like adorning a tree with lights at Christmastime made her think that an intuition of some other realm wasn't completely gone from us; that humans still felt something, that there was still something to honour. People wanted to lift themselves up and lift up their neighbours with these silly little adornments—which to her, the winter her father died, meant so much. She walked through her neighbourhood, choked up with gratitude over all those tiny shining souls that adorned the trees and the falling-down porches. Humans knew! They remembered! These lights spoke to our knowledge of another world, the world behind this world, the world of the spirit. Nobody was thinking it, but they knew it, nonetheless. Humans hadn't lost what was most beautiful; our very small and tentative sense of the hidden, magnificent, divine. No one said it, but buried in their hearts, there it was.

These little lights, strung across all the trees, proved it. We knew so little about who we were, or what we were doing here, but this little gesture spoke so gently of our not-knowing, our hope, our sense of connection to something universally shared—which was our not-knowing, so magnificent and dizzyingly deep. It was her most reliable comfort in those winter months, when her heart was bare. It was the only thing that warmed her. *I always found them cheap*, a woman at a party said. *Yes, of course*, she replied. *I did, too.* But she wanted to explain that she finally understood them, and saw through their cheapness to their deeper beauty. But how could she say what she meant? That people had placed these bright, sparkling, colourful souls everywhere, on every tree and on every doorstep; they reassured her that people knew that all around us, in the air and in the trees, were the colourful, sparkling souls of the dead. These bright and twinkling spots of light shining out from the darkness were all of their ancestors, now her own father, and all the people who had ever been born and died. We strung these symbols of them across our own houses in our knowledge of their living and dying, relieved to have them twinkling near, with us here forever.

Only once in her life, lying in bed with her dying father, was she actually where she was, and not imagining she was somewhere she would rather have been. Then, when the spirit of her father went into her, it felt like her one true experience of life, since it was not something she had invented or pursued.

And she knew if she had to live one moment over forever, that is the moment that she'd choose, and everything else could vanish.

THREE

Decades ago, on a beautiful summer day, upon an old water-logged tree, Mira sat with her father, and was warmed by the light of the sun. What was she hoping to find if she returned to that spot? She just wanted a little peace in her heart. She wondered if being there would bring her back to life, but none of their good, earlier feelings returned as she sat there, only her failure at not having made things right with him.

She threw her heart out. She threw out her brain, her arms, her hair, her feet; she threw all of herself into the water, hoping the lake would catch her, save her, hold her, and return her refreshed to the shore. It did not.

~

She went down to the water, stripped off her clothes, and went in. It was cold. She had once feared swimming in it. As kids, they had been told that the water was polluted. But then when they got older, the adults said no, it wasn't polluted and it never had been.

She must have transformed as the sunlight shone down onto the earth like a golden ball, or the tides must have washed her back onto the shore, under a branch, which is where some part of her rose up, up, up into a leaf in a tree.

One day the lake would flood the whole city from the ice caps melting into the sea, and the whole city would be destroyed, and anyone she had ever called a friend, and that log, and this leaf, and everyone.

~

She was drawn up into a leaf in a tree by the lake where there was a small cluster of trees near the sand. The log beneath it had been broken off in a storm and had washed up and lodged there below it—very old, waterlogged, and finally dry; it was used as a bench by many people, and it had been used as a bench for years.

It was on this log that she had sat with her father, who she had loved perhaps more than she had loved anyone. They had sat looking out at the lake, at the condo towers as they were being built. But the first time they sat by the water, no towers had yet been built. Back then, long ago, there was nothing by the water but seaweed and pop bottles washed up on the sand.

~

As soon as she was in the leaf, she knew she had made a mistake. She had wanted to go to a better place, but her spirit got caught in a leaf. That it could be contained within a leaf made her wonder at how small her spirit was, when she had been so sure, in life, that her spirit was huge.

She was caught in the leaf, and inside her there was an awareness that something had gone wrong. There, beneath her, people were strolling, people who didn't look up at a leaf. Even if they had looked up, could she have conveyed her message? She could not communicate with the other leaves. Were there spirits trapped in them, too? How much lonelier she was in the leaf than she had been as a person, anywhere.

Soon she couldn't remember what her problems in life had been. What had made her so sad and guilty that the solution was to go into a leaf? Then there was the frustration of having no legs, so no way to walk away from this new life, this position in the universe. Now she could do nothing but convert sunlight into food, and even that wasn't very much fun.

You were supposed to have a secret wish to get you where you wanted to go. She had also had a secret wish, but it had been such a secret that she didn't know what its words would be; she only knew what it felt like. The secret wish turned out to be *leaf*. Everything she had wanted came down to *leaf*, and she hadn't even known it.

As a leaf, she finally found her right dimensions, and soon enough she adapted to them, as she had never adapted to her dimensions in life. The problem in life had always been that she had wanted to be bigger, but didn't know how. She could not adapt to her right size. She didn't even know what her right size was. But there, under the golden sun, she finally found out: it was the size of a leaf. If she had been told this when she was a child, she could have adapted to it, and led a simple life of little striving, and been happy, rather than hoping and attending school. But the love of her father had made her think she was great, as giant as the universe, and that other people should know it. What had she accomplished with all her ambition to prove his beliefs about her right?

Instead, she might have been content with choosing one person to love, and living with them simply, someone who was also the size of a leaf, rather than the size of the shore. Perhaps this was where she had first gone wrong: in thinking she could be the size of a shore, and letting her father hope that for her, rather than telling him, *No.* He had been so excited, encouraging her in his certainty that she was the size of the shore, or could be. He had expended much energy on her, and what had that gotten him in return? She had gone into the world without him, thinking she could achieve it, but she had achieved only a strange distance from this person she loved. If she had known that she was the size of a leaf, she would not have bothered with those aspirations. She would have done her best to remain small.

She hadn't known that plants were the grateful recipients of all consciousness—not only of people, but of snails and squirrels and the sun and the rain; that it was their generosity that made them so lush and green, the very colour of welcome. Was every tree so peppered with the consciousness of snails and squirrels and people and bees? And what will happen to her in the autumn? Is that when she will really be dead? No, perhaps then she'll retreat into the trunk of the tree. Perhaps that's what makes trees so magnificent: that as generous and accepting as their leaves are, their trunk is even more accepting. It welcomes one and all. Then the tree will let her slip out again, back through its branches as it buds in the spring. But what if the tree is cut down? Perhaps she'll go into the next tree, then she'll go into the next one, and she'll just keep on going—into the soil or whatever's left; particles from a distant sun.

Is her father in this leaf with her? That is, his spirit—is it in here with her? Are she and her father in this leaf together, or is she all alone? Did his spirit, coming into her body when he died, bind with hers forever, or did it leave her body soon after it entered?

Can she detect her father in this leaf? Yes, she can. *Father, are you there? If you are, can you answer me?*

Her father answers: he is here. But he doesn't want to talk. His peace is greater than hers is. Peace means truly no talking. Doesn't he want to return to life? He enjoyed it, he loved it, it's over, it's fine. He does not want to return to life. He has nothing more to live for there. He likes it here—in this quiet. His human life was full of so many troubles, as a human life always is—the troubles of the body, and of people who are pains in the neck. Who needs it? She does. She thinks she needs it still. *Father, will you come back with me?* Her father is gentle, but he doesn't want to. He wishes her well, if that's what she wants to do. Does she want to? Yes. She wants to resume human living. She wants to begin all over again. She wants to be someone's baby.

Her father says it doesn't work that way. Unless a baby is born under a tree. But what if a baby is strolled under the tree, sleeping or pushed in a stroller? Can't she go into a baby then? *Oh yes*, her father says, *I guess you could. But you shouldn't.*

She knows it.

Don't go into a baby, her father implies. She knows that he is right.

It takes a certain discipline to be dead. She never had much discipline. Her father, in the leaf, displays utter discipline, or maybe he just doesn't want to go back.

~

Father, do you really need me to be in this leaf with you?

He says he does not.

Then why did I come here? Why did I do this?

He doesn't answer. He was dead when she did it. He didn't do it to her.

In the beginning, her father wanted to stay quiet, simple, strong and apart. They were in the same leaf, that was all. They had discovered each other, but the discovery led to nothing. It was simply a presence, a flatness, and a feeling that the other was near. It was acknowledged without being talked about.

In life, things always have to be undergone to stamp a closeness between two people. But in a leaf, there is no question of betrayal, so there is no question of trust. There they were, day in, day out, in the leaf together.

Being the more restless, she was the one who kept trying to have conversations. At first, he wouldn't carry his side. He would say one thing in his stillness, and there was no inflection in his voice, no change of tone. It was not the youthful voice of her father that she remembered, but something much more leaflike.

I still can't imagine entanglement. You know what entanglement says? No. Two particles are somehow related and they—oh yeah. Even at a distance. And one of them changes, and then the other one changes. Instantaneously. How is that possible? That makes no sense. How does information pass between them? I guess there must be some other realm, the realm of the mind or consciousness that they're both a part of. Wait, what does the mind have to do with it? I don't know, what do minds have to do with it? Nothing, because there were no minds when the universe first began. We don't know. Consciousness is a huge mystery, and no one understands how consciousness arises from a brain. No? No, just the fact of a brain, and the leap from a brain, which keeps the heart pumping, to self-consciousness is not something people understand. But just because they don't understand it, doesn't mean it's complicated. I'm not saying it's complicated, I'm saying it's a mystery. Well, I don't think it's a significant mystery. Because you're not interested in it, but I'm more interested in the mystery of consciousness than in the first few seconds of how the world began. You are? But animals are conscious, a dog is conscious. Yeah, and I include that in the mystery of consciousness. But even a worm is conscious. Right, it makes a decision whether to turn this way or that way. Even cells have something akin to free will, and single-cell organisms, they too have to decide whether to go this way or that way. Exactly. And there's macrophages and things within the body that make their own decisions, and they can make the decision to shut you down. Right, there's a kind of vanity to thinking you're the only decider, or that making good decisions will keep you alive, because your cells are making decisions, too. Sure, I think a person should enjoy themselves instead of worrying about whether they're going to live to ninety-one or ninety-two. Yeah, who cares. My basic premise is that in life, you live forever, because as soon as you die, you don't realize you're dead, so you're kind of always alive, so the thing is, you shouldn't worry about yourself. The only ones to worry about are the people you leave behind who might have needed you. Right, like if you have little children or something. But otherwise? I mean, a hundred and fifty thousand people die in the world every day. That's a huge number, and life goes on. It's not a big tragedy, so it's not worth worrying about. Yeah, and I mean, what's the alternative? Well, there is no alternative. That's what I'm saying, what's the alternative? What those programmers want to do? Download your brain into the computer so that you can be a program? And then they come and unplug you or something? I know, it sounds like a horror show. I can't believe this is something people want. Well, it's because they don't understand the fact that you live forever, and when you die, you don't regret it. You don't sit up there saying, *Oh man, if only I could be at the ball game, why can't I be at the ball game*. Right, that makes no sense. And they say that Christianity solved it because you can live forever, but you might go to hell forever, so that's really sick.

And something that goes on forever? Who'd want that? Who'd want to live something over and over again, or to be stuck being a farmer for a thousand years? What do you mean, being a farmer for a thousand years? Well, let's say you could live for a thousand years. But why a farmer? Well, if you happen to be a farmer, but whatever, a teacher, a mechanic, a chef. Why do they even want to live forever? To look at photos of things they're not even a part of? Who cares? Or to be friends with two hundred people? And get one hundred or two hundred things on your feed each day? What kind of life is that for a thousand years?

Then she could hear him as she had in life, with the natural buoyancy that marked him as her youthful and ever-loving father. She had made him speak! It had been a shyness that had kept her from making him speak in the early days or weeks of being in the leaf with him. He had taken on a sort of majesty or a magnificence in having been dead before her. His relation was to something larger now, whereas before his relation had been mainly to her.

She could tell from how long it took him to speak that the peace of death was simple for him to inhabit, and left no other desires.

~

Then a happy pleasure roused him from his peace, to have her back again, close to him.

In a leaf, talking happens without mouths. You don't need two separate bodies to talk. You can speak to one another from within the same vein, from within the same flesh. One leaf can hold two minds and two points of view.

How do you draw a father out of his rest? She just said all

the stupid things that had bothered him in their human life. It became impossible for him to let her say the things that he had once found so irrational. So she made him forget his perfect peace, and drew him halfway back.

Because you know what, if we suddenly went back two thousand years, there'd be nothing we could do to speed things along. I don't know how to make a steam engine. We'd not be much help as time travellers. We'd be useless. I know, I know. That's why everybody should learn enough so that if they ever went back a thousand years, they could speed up history. That'd be really depressing to go back with no useful skills. I don't know enough chemistry, I don't know enough anything, I couldn't build an airplane, I couldn't build a car. Almost nobody could. Huh? None of us could. Yeah, well, some people could. I wouldn't even know how to smelt iron. How do you find iron? How do you build a smelter? They're doing that in two thousand, three thousand BC. The first metal they had was copper. You just smelt it and it's there. Then bronze, which is copper and tin, just in case you ever need to know. And you know where you found tin? In England. So if I return to a thousand years ago, I'll just go to England and find tin. Then Crete became a power because they figured out how to make bronze. What's so great about having bronze? It's a much harder metal, so you could make better weapons with it. Right, right, I guess that was the bronze age. Then came the iron age where they found iron and learned to smelt iron, which had to be done at a higher temperature. I wonder if they knew that they were in that age. Well, they didn't call it the bronze age, they called it modern times. I know they didn't call it the bronze age. A human has to eat, to build shelter, to clothe themselves. There's nothing easy about doing that without any tools. Isn't it nice not to have hands? Yes, it's a relief. With hands you feel you must do something with them, and be doing something with them all the time. That's what it felt like to have two hands. The nice thing about not having hands is not to feel the requirement. Do you love it? I like it. I didn't realize that bodies are what give us urges. When you have parts, they make you want to use them. What is the part that makes us want to love someone who doesn't love us back? Don't focus on that. What should I focus on, then? That the probability of any person being around is one in a trillion, so it's almost a zero percent chance of you being here. But you're going to have, you know, eight billion people, and those eight billion people have won the lottery. And the worst part is that nobody realizes that! They don't realize what a rare opportunity they have to observe this universe, because here's this amazing universe, and if humans hadn't evolved to this stage, they wouldn't know they were living in this beautiful place. You know they've found a bacterium which can extend life by twenty-five percent? Whoa! They've done it in mice. In mice? Why are mice so lucky?? Why do people care so much about mice!? I'll never understand.

The whole surface of the lake was a giant, watery eyeball, taking in the sky and the clouds and all the people who were walking up along the boardwalk and down along the shore. But people forgot that the lake was an open eyeball. Mira could see that they came here because they wanted privacy, but they forgot that they were being seen by the lake.

～

Those beautiful days when she and her father were in the leaf! The sleepy peacefulness of the lake at night, soothing and lulling them with its dreams; and the dreams she had in the leaf were unlike any dreams she'd had as a human, since they came from the tree and returned to the tree, travelling through its veins.

And the books on her shelf and her father's shelf? She remembers they had books, without recalling their names. All the reading they had done in the hopes of transporting themselves, a transporting that finally happened with death, which delivered them the transporting they had hoped for by reading, while fearing it in the form of death—all while longing for it in reading!

You can philosophize about God all you like, that doesn't make him real. I know, all I'm trying to say is that if you want to have a true picture of God in your head, you have to recognize that you can have no true picture of him. Of course not! Of course you can't have a true picture of something that doesn't exist. But if you *believed* that God existed. Then you can believe anything you want, because if you believe in God, God is something that can do or be anything it wants to be, so it can be a million things, it can be different for everybody. That doesn't make it not real; that might make it even more real, like a fingerprint is different on every human body, or the way our muscles work has a unique signature, too—so does that make a fingerprint, or the way our muscles work, something that's not real? Look, it's against the laws of nature. They say God put the whole universe into motion, but how can he do that without a physical being?— because it's a basic thing. For something to act, it has to have a physical being. But cells act and you can't see cells, and atoms act and you can't see atoms. Yes you can, you can see them through a microscope. But without a microscope we couldn't see them. I know, so what? So all I'm saying is that maybe we don't have the technology yet to see God. No! Well, we once didn't have the technology to see cells or atoms. But humans had an inkling, even before we could see them, that such things were there, that small things made up big things. But they couldn't prove it, and humans have always had an inkling of God, too. You must admit, we don't understand completely how the universe works. I agree, we don't know what dark energy is, and we don't know what dark matter is, and it makes up eighty percent of the universe. Right, we're discovering things all the time. I know, but those are details. Eighty percent of the universe is not a detail! I know, but they'll eventually figure it out, and when they do figure it out, it'll make sense, because things make sense. But what I'm saying is that maybe it's not even that there are *things* we don't know, but that our minds are not good enough that we ever *can* know. Come on. Or because maybe if there is a God, we're conceiving of him wrong, and that's why we can't find him. Are you being serious or just being provocative? No, I'm not being provocative. You're being serious. I don't know, I'm not a thousand percent sure like you are, because I don't think the scientific method is the only way to prove that something is real. No? What do you think is the way to prove that something is real? Imagination. Imagination is not a proof! Well, I just think not everything has a logical explanation. Well, it has either a logical explanation or an illogical explanation.

Then Annie came to sit under the tree. Mira didn't know how she'd found it. Perhaps she was drawn to it by the forces of nature, or perhaps she was drawn here by Mira. She must have found it restful, with Mira's love shining down on her, and the love of whoever was in the tree.

Mira was so excited to see Annie there! She wanted to tell her everything she knew. Something monstrous, and then what? Something great. A party where there wasn't a party, and plants where there were no plants. And the plants will take over everything, pushing through the concrete and growing up the walls. The tendrils of the plants and the grasses and vines will line the empty pools, whose concrete will be breaking, and the green will come through, and the soil will come through, and the rains will come down, and all the buildings will start tumbling down. It's to let the green plants live that so many of our structures will have to die. The plants will be everywhere in the second draft of life, and they will have a sublime slowness, and a happy peace. The ruthless plants will make way for the gentle ones, and none of life will be so ruthless in the second draft of life. They will decorate the earth and all the crumbled buildings and all of existence. Purple flowers, scented sweet, roses and yellow flowers, and yellow roses and white ones. The entire earth will be a garden sprouting forth, open-ing with the sun and closing with the moon, and the plants will not remember how we cut them in the first draft. The vegetables will tell no stories. They won't recall the pots, or being plucked and eaten. They will have a happy innocence which plants in the first draft have not.

In the cosmic landscape, plants have front-row seats. God is thrilled to have the audience of creation made up mostly of plant life: trees and bushes, flowers and berries, sitting down to enjoy the show, and saying at intermission, *What a romp!*

But for us to imagine ourselves in their place would be utterly horrifying to the humans, who would not want to be living that way: life as an eternity of enjoying plays! But the plants have learned, over millions of years, how to be the audience of creation. They know how good it feels to be the open, accepting audience of the show, which humans could never be, and wouldn't even understand, for our purpose comes from being its critics.

Seeing an audience of plants just sitting there seems like doom and uselessness to a human. But to be the audience of creation is a wonderful thing. What a privilege to be able to sit there and watch it! To be entirely filled up by life's beauty! It's a privilege to have front-row seats. But it was not easy for the plants to learn how to sit there.

For what reason are they tasked with being the audience of creation? Oh, for no reason. Oh, because God is an egoist. Because he is an artist. Because even though creation is flawed, God is secretly proud of its aspects, and loves his work being noticed.

Well, *you* worry about an asteroid hitting the earth in the next million years. Who does? You do. No I don't. I just think it's amazing that these objects which are way out there are really not so far away, and that they can actually have an impact on the earth. I mean, you think about the solar system as being fairly stable except for the occasional asteroid coming by, but you don't think of a sun coming into our solar system and disrupting it—but it could! A million years is not that far away, and it's going to go through the Oort cloud. What's the Oort cloud? It's these small rocky bodies way outside our solar system, but surrounding our solar system. But not encircling it? Yes, a sphere around our solar system. A cloud of rocks? A cloud of rocks of various sizes, and supposedly another sun is going to go through that, and it's going to disrupt our orbit, and some of it is going to come into the solar system and shower the earth and cause all kinds of destruction. But then I was thinking, What if that sun has its *own* Oort cloud?—then *its* Oort cloud is going to go right through us, which is a much more direct hit. Every sun doesn't have its own Oort cloud, does it? Probably does. If ours does, why wouldn't every other sun have it? Is it the gravitational pull of the sun that creates the Oort cloud? When a solar system forms, there's all kinds of debris, and things are going around a central point of gravity and the centre collapses into a sun, and then other things collapse into planets, and some of it is so far away that it's not quite pulled in, so it continues going around and around. So it orbits? Not only that, but its planets are going to be interacting with our planets. It's going to be a big mess! And for sure that's going to happen? Yes, I mean it's heading this way. I mean, in a million years, people will start to worry about it. If there still are people. Well, I think there will always be people; the question for the future is, at what level of civilization, and how many people? Because I can see civilization collapsing and going back to subsistence farming. Why? Wars over water and stuff? Yes, this order collapsing and ninety percent of the people die. But what happens to hydro plants? That's what I mean, people are going to have to go back to what they had before. But why won't there be electricity? Because to have electricity, you need a critical mass of people, and money and knowledge, and if there are twenty people left in a city, you're not going to be able to run a hydroelectric plant. Right. I think it's so dumb, people planning colonies on Mars. They should be planning things here, figuring out how to live *here*. Well, they think it's a mess so they want to go somewhere pure. But it's pure nothing! They want to transform Mars so it will be like the earth, instead of trying to make the best of this place! Well, it's tedious for people. It's tedious for people? What is? To try and correct their mistakes. But it's so much easier than making a new earth. You'll go to Mars and live in a bubble? And you can never go fishing, and you can never go swimming, and you can never go boating, and you can never go out? Maybe they will figure out how to make

117

big bodies of water. But it will take a thousand years, because the atmosphere has to build up. Right, eventually Mars will warm up, and the ice will melt and will form lakes and rivers. But it's going to be a thousand years. And it will never be like the earth.

The most delicate leaves, green and humble and finally fading, who not one person pays attention to, but who nevertheless thrive in silence, beneath the sinking sun. Mira wonders if leaves exist in the human heart. Do they exist in Annie's heart?

Mira watched Annie walk around with another woman, who was prettier and more graceful than Mira had been, and she felt that this woman wanted something from Annie, and that Annie would definitely give it to her. It was something warmer than what Mira had wanted. She felt that this woman was more pleasing to Annie, and more pleasing was what this woman wanted, too. Because of that, she felt sure that Annie was going to give it to her. Mira was going to be the one who didn't get what she wanted, while this woman would. Their voices were warm and tender and close. They had come down to the water for privacy, and perhaps for other reasons that Mira couldn't know. Or perhaps Annie had come knowing that Mira was there, to show her that she could give something to someone that she had never given to Mira, because Mira hadn't known how to draw it out of her, or because she had not been smart or tender enough to know, or for some other reason.

When it became late, they left the shore, and Mira couldn't see them anymore.

The grandfather of the shapes the square, the circle, the triangle and the orange—that's what you have to look forward to. And other things like that? Yes, other things like that. A whole magnificent conservation of energy. A drain on all your resources. And the fact that people as you know them won't be here for the second draft of existence. Why's that? Because not everything is given the same each time. What would be given to humans the same each time is exactly what is given to all life on earth, and that is the beautiful thing that is loved. It will still be here in the next draft of existence, and it will be here in whatever evolves that is like humans, if anything does. Evolution can go many ways. I think the thing you're sad about is that our art won't be appreciated by the woolly mammoths. That's okay; I have thought about it and it's clear to me now that art is made for our situation. Whatever comes will be another situation, and our art won't be needed for it. So that's not sad? No, it's not sad for things to be useful in their time, art included. The birds might have beautiful pictures on the walls of their nests. No one has ever climbed a tree to see. No, the point is that birds in the next situation might not even need paintings. But it's true, there's nothing to be sad about. When you are sad about the humans being gone, it's the art you think of that won't be seen, not the humans, who maybe don't deserve to be here, because they are so killing. You have love in you, but that part is extra-human, and that part is in the plants, and the animals, and the clouds, and the seas, and everything. What is lovable is not humans, but life. And life will always be here? Yes, there are cycles, and if the earth gets sick, it will get well again, in maybe a million or two billion years. It will do what it needs to, because it is self-correcting in the fullness of time. So the humans evolved, and they evolved as killing creatures in so many ways, willing to torture, and self-involved. Then why not get rid of the humans, if what we love about humans is everywhere on earth, and is not exclusive to humans, which is the ability to love, which runs at an angle to everything else about us? It is amazing that these things co-exist, but they do. And when you see it happening in a person, the love that is there, then a person can be as lovable as a plant, or a cat. Then you can love a person as you loved me. And as you loved me. But there is so much not to love. Of course, that is the way humans evolved, and it's not the worst thing that humans will be gone. We are the tragic ones who think it's a tragedy that the human animal will be gone. We can't even accept that our own fathers will be gone! But that doesn't mean it's a tragedy on a worldwide scale. Except for all the suffering. Except for all the suffering, but then the earth will start doing what it's already doing, which is making itself well again. We are part of its flu. That means we will all be somewhere else, at least the part of us that loves. The part of the earth that is pure love, that exists in humans and animals, will still be here after the humans are gone, and evolution repopulates the earth with twice the number of birds, or whatever comes to replace birds. That will be God making the next draft? Or will that be evolution? I don't know, it's all the same to me. Yes, where you are there is the ease of saying, *It's all the same to me.* But there are those of us who are still here with the living and the dying. But not for long! I'm sure there is a beauty to being dead, and to being just love, and whatever was best about you being all that's left. I can say that it is very relaxing. In fact, that's the nicest thing about it, to shed what evolution made us, remarkable creatures, yet so killing. And to shed what God needs from us, remarkable creatures, yet so critiquing. I am looking forward to it, to my critiquing and killing being gone, and to having the love part being all that remains. Why are people so afraid of it? They *like* the killing part of themselves! They think it's the best thing about them! To criticize sometimes becomes joined with killing and winning. Look at the ones who are winning: they are the walking dead. The part that wants to win is made through evolution, and the part that wants to criticize is our important function, from God. They are both at an angle to the loving part, which gets smaller and smaller in time, as the killing and winning part is grown. It is hard for these two parts not to bear down on the loving part. So I shouldn't feel bad when I am not winning? No, just be glad you're not the walking dead. There were shows about them once, about people who walked the earth, half-dead. Because those creatures really do exist! That is the thing about life, is that you want to feel the loving part, but the winning part becomes bound up with criticizing and killing—not only others, but yourself. I'm sure I can step back from the winning and killing part. But you cannot step back from the criticizing part, and you're not supposed to. You were very loving to me, and I only remember the loving parts of you now. That is true when someone dies—that you often only think about the loving part, but in that way you are just thinking about life, which runs through plants and trees; the loving part which is part of everything. That part of us is the best thing about us, and because it is the least individual thing, it shines through us so beautifully, when it shines. It is easy to remember that part, which is equivalent with life, when the person you love is dead. The winning parts are equivalent with death. You only remember the loving parts, which are life, in order to bring me back to life. When you remember the criticizing and killing parts, you are not as sad about my death. That was my death in life, too. It is not a mistake to remember this. It is not bad to remember the parts of my life that were death. But it is better and easier to remember the parts that were life, because while the winning and critiquing part dies, the loving part goes somewhere else; it still remains somewhere. How beautifully love lights up the person in life! How love truly illuminates us! Yes, and whatever illuminated them is somewhere else now, illuminating something else. When you remember me in a loving way, it is the thing that illuminates everything on earth that is shining through your memories. So why don't you focus on the memories that make you happy, the beautiful ones, for that recalls the light which shone through me, and which is the same as the light that shines through you. I am sad the first draft is coming to an end, but I mustn't cry for all of existence, or for the art that will no longer be understood. For it's okay, it was understood when the situation required it. And don't forget the birds that will be replacing these birds when the earth or God gets it right. And those future birds might be like our present birds, or unlike our birds, but they will sing, and they will have pictures on the walls of their nests, however large those nests are; and who is to say that those pictures will not be as beautiful, or even more beautiful, than our best artists can make? And it will be excitingly new, a situational art for the situation that those birds, or birdlike creatures, will find themselves in. We will always find ourselves in a situation. And a million or a half a million years from now—it is hard to know how numbers work—a situation will still be happening. How I would love to come back and see what the new art of those new birds will be! But you *will* be back, and you will always be here. Don't think that in death you go far from the earth; you remain down here with everything— the part of you that loved, which is the most important part. That part of you will patiently be here as the earth changes colour, exhausts itself, breathes in fresh life again, and revives. That part of you will be here all along, through that whole entire time, while the slugs make their sluggish art, beautiful little swirls in the mud, and whatever will populate the sea, and the greatest beasts that will ever be; slippery with green gills and lots of scales, feathers and fur. Even the swimming creatures will have their own ways of moving which will be radically new. And you will be here for that, too! Why am I so stuck in the art of the past? Because you are stuck in this situation, thinking it is the only one. There will be a second draft, and the part of you that loves, which is the best part of you, and the most eternal part, will be in the bears, the lizards, the mammoths, and the birds, there in the second draft of life. You are sad because art, which is love, will be gone, but you only need art because you are stuck in the first draft. You are sad because your father had to die, but in the next draft you won't be sad, because there won't be fathers.

Then Mira could sense Annie from inside the leaf, walking with that woman who was maybe her girlfriend, and they were speaking so confidentially. Mira strained to hear what they were saying, but they never came close enough for her to hear. Or perhaps a leaf is designed in many beautiful ways, but not to know the words. Mira and her father continued to speak while Mira strained to hear Annie. What words of love had Annie learned to say in the time that had passed since their school days? Mira could sense their shadowy outlines, silhouetted against the lake. When their voices grew excited, and when their voices lowered, something stirred inside of Mira. Her father couldn't feel it. He had never met Annie.

Mira knew that one day Annie would leave the shore, and that she would never return to find Mira. And then what would Mira do with her love—with the heat that as a leaf she could so subtly send off, send off as a warm nothing into the air? But she couldn't remember any longer whether humans could feel it.

One night, when there was just a moon in a cloudless sky, Annie returned again with that same woman. Something glinted off that woman's hair so beautifully, and the pain of this beauty made Mira want not to see. She understood that Annie no longer loved her, if she ever had—although perhaps she still did, even if it was in some way Annie did not understand, for she kept on returning to sit near her tree. Mira knew she shouldn't call it *her* tree, like it was hers.

What you want are fixers, but what is needed is to follow the traditions with faith. You want people to come in and fix things for you, to show you what the fixes are. But what is needed is to follow the family traditions. Getting together for meals. Faith that this matters. Follow the traditions with love. Being sent to earth in a million hot years. Meanwhile, with all the non-people, eating cheese crisps and mildly playing cards or sitting on chairs, waiting for the soul's one chance at a human life on earth, where they will find their truest love. Two are meant to find each other, and they do. It might be a million hot years before you are made to live again, but that is not so long, and it feels like nothing to wait. It's amazing out here, near Saturn, the blackness and the rightness and patience of everything, and not having any desires. It's possible to live that way for a million hot years, and without desire, it goes fast and leisurely. It takes the right amount of time. Then, on earth, to meet your true love on the cast of a TV show—what a surprise that it would happen like that! That must mean TV is important in some way, if two people could be set up to meet on the set of a TV show. TV must truly be an eternal way of telling stories, so the universe let us evolve to have TV. There are so many things you can do with your body if you can let it relax and bend to the shape of the universe, which is spherical tubes that are spherical not only in one direction, such as along it, but within it at every juncture, so that you can bend your back over the sphere of Saturn's rings, not only sideways across the ring but within the ring itself, which is spherical all the way through. Part of human life is following the traditions of family. That's part of the real plot of it. If you follow the traditions, you don't need fixers, who will kill you eventually. I should never have let them into my house, but I did it because my child was having problems, and a smart person saw the connection between the littlest person and the biggest one, and they thought the problem had to do with attention, so the usual solutions in that scenario were sought, and the fixers were brought in. But even as the fixers were being brought in, the awareness was washing over me that they were not going to help, even as all the evidence that they would help, and could help, was being lined up. What was needed was to follow the family traditions, which included not eating sweets before dinner. *Why not?* asked the child, who wanted to eat the cake first. And all that was needed was to gently say, *Because that's not how it's done.* So it's the same thing with family life; that the traditions are apparent, and that they are there in the very fabric of a family. One might be tempted to ask, *What are the traditions?* But that is not what is needed; to ask, *What are the traditions?* What is needed is to follow them with faith, with the faith that following them is enough. If you follow, you don't need to ask what they are.

They are kindness and family get-togethers, for instance. They are everyone being in the same room. They are an openness to other people, and keeping the fixers out. The fixers are coming from the world of psychology, from those who know nothing about the traditions and don't care, and would smash them if they could, and would institute a whole series of reforms. They don't know the law of a person being brought to earth after a million hot years, and that they are brought here for a simple reason—to follow the family traditions. You don't even have to ask what they are. If you are asking, you have no faith. Doing causes the knowledge of it. The family was set up by whatever force brings one to live a human life, finally after a million hot years. It is not a coincidence who we encounter here, or who is put inside the family. There is no point in asking what a family is. If you follow the traditions, you know it. The dark stratosphere apart from human life is a place of nothing to fear. There is nothing to fear about being so far away from the earth or its people or its ways. Few go wrong in the stratosphere. And on earth, few of its people go wrong, because it is in the knowledge of a human that they were sent to earth to follow the family traditions. The family needs to be together, and together, that is the helping. Bringing in fixers is not a solution, because they will kill the family eventually. A family that is brought together by the universe doesn't need fixers. Fixers were invented on earth by people who wanted to be fixers, so they must not become part of the family, because only people who do not have faith would bring in the fixers. A family isn't made for no reason at all. The reason is because a human life, which we are brought to earth to experience about every million years, allows for the structure of a life with faith. A family emerges from the mystery of life; it emerges from the ether. There is not nothingness way out here, after life, where there is no gravity, and the laws of the universe and the laws of physics are not as you experience them there on earth. That does not mean that those laws are better, but you have to not have fear; if you relax into them, then you will see that the laws that exist out here, post-life, in the dark universe, are a lot of fun. People who like roller coasters have some sense of the speed and the dizziness of the fun, but your body is not confined to a track, for instead of a track it's the rings of Saturn. You might be asked, *Do you want to experience it?* And the answer is, *Yes*, but then you have to relax. The universe, having let you die, is not going to kill you again. It takes some time to get used to this, that you are not going to keep on dying, and that there's a new place to be in, a place without friends or desire or family. In the stratosphere, with all this blackness, the feeling of living is a different thing; life is not set upon by a human body, but it might *look* like bodies are sitting about at little round tables, on plastic stools, playing cards, and it might *look* like there are little capsule-closets that are used as bathrooms. It might look it, but what matters are the adventures you find here, in the life in which there is no death; the adventures of speed, bending, dizziness, and the different philosophical and physical rules. It really is amazing, and you do hear gossip, like, *They did not believe they would find their true love on the set of a TV show*, and you do hear gossip from the universe, like, *They are going to be brought to earth in a million hot years.* And you can see the damage of the fixers, and how they have to be killed, but are unkillable. They won't rest, because once they are brought into a family, they won't die, and once they have been let in, they will always be there, in the room when you're not looking. But you don't need fixers if you follow the traditions. But it's not until after death that a person knows that this is what they were asked. We did a pretty good job, didn't we? You think we did? Did we not bring in the fixers? I don't remember the fixers. Maybe there were fixers. If there were fixers, there couldn't have been more than one or two. A person only brings in fixers when they cannot follow with faith; when they lose the ability to do so, or when they don't have the desire to do so. The family must attend to its own problems, not fix them, but be in them together, by following the traditions with faith. Is that what we are doing? Is that what this is? I don't know. I only know what the traditions are when I'm not asking, *That begs the question, what are the traditions?* I met that cousin of yours who you never liked, and though I doubted you when you were alive, it turns out you were right all along: he was a complete jerk. That's one way of putting it. He didn't follow the traditions with faith. What are the traditions? Just love and interest in the family. Him not inviting you to his home when you travelled to his country, over there across the world; that was not following the traditions. I often doubted you when you said something bad about a person in the family, thinking that the problem was with you. You also had criticisms of me, and just as I doubted the things you said about others—I was always suspicious and taking their side—I doubted your criticisms of me, too, but you were right. I see that because you were right about the rest. You were not criticizing too harshly, and what made you criticize was how it felt—how other humans treated you. Is that how we know whether we are following the traditions of the human family? How we make others feel? Oh, that might be part of it. I'm sorry for when I did not follow the traditions with faith. I'm sorry for all those times I went and brought in fixers. The fixers didn't help us. They drew me away from the family traditions, and they drew me away from you. I will hopefully see you again in a million hot years. Is that how it works? I don't know. I only got a glimpse of that faraway place. I have not heard enough of its gossip.

Then Annie was telling this woman that her life would change again and again, but that she would never know these changes as they occurred, but that was one thing about life we had to believe in, and that was transformation. The woman had just moved to a small town, so she knew something about that. The town was small, but if she tried, Annie said, she could maybe make it small enough—small enough to do something there that would matter. Then Annie pointed out two swans that were swimming in the lake together. There was a grey swan and a white one. *Every person belongs to our great social life*, Annie was saying, *so you are like those two swans, but in one body. A person is both those swans, don't you see?* Then the swans dipped their heads under the water, for it made them shy to be talked about; everyone always forgets this about the swans. *The grey swan is your body*, Annie was saying, *and the white swan is our communal life. See how they swim together? How lonely would that grey swan be, if the white swan went and left it.* Then the woman started to cry. She didn't want the grey swan that was her body to leave the white swan that was our communal life, or to have to swim without it. *They must swim together*, Annie said. Then Mira remembered that Annie had never had parents, while Mira had a father, and here she was, trapped with him in a leaf. She was still a child. Annie had grown up more completely than Mira had, for Annie had never had parents, so it was easier for her to enter communal life, and even to know it existed. But Mira had her father, so she never had to. Having her father had kept her a child in a childhood home, but Mira had made a big mistake, following her father into death, as though *she* was her body, and *he* was communal life. Her body was meant to stay with the swan that *really was* our communal life! Her life wasn't supposed to go with him! What had she done in coming into a leaf? And would the universe, which had its own laws, ever forgive her for distorting them?

Then at the same time, she was screaming to get out, calling, *Annie! Annie!* A voice beside her was saying, *But how do you know she will hear us?* But she knew this voice was just telling her lies! If Mira screamed, Annie would hear her, and she would get her out. She just had to scream loud enough, above the whole entire din that is inside a leaf. She knew that Annie would get her out if she could hear her. She screamed until her voice was lost, then she tried not to be too scared of the logic that was trying to keep her there, reasoning with her endlessly, for she knew it was just trying to frighten her. It was scaring her by trying to reassure her, so Mira began to pull the electricity out. But that only felt like it was trapping her deeper in that underground place. Everything she was doing was trapping her more, and she didn't know why it was so scary all of a sudden, when it hadn't been scary before. No one anywhere could hear her or cared! The leaf's walls seemed to be made of concrete, and she was deep inside it, scary and dark with bright-coloured lights, and everyone was oblivious to her screams. How had her screaming not worked to get her out of there? *Annie! Annie!* She had been sure that someone could hear her from way outside the leaf, but now she was not so sure. If only she had started screaming before, before the whole entire thing enveloped her. There was evil, fright, scariness and hatred down there, and the longer she was in it, the longer she would stay. She had no sense of where the exit was, she saw no stairs, no elevator going up; the place was designed to keep you. There'd be no getting out. She would have to go through the whole entire thing of letting the voice scare her and scare her and scare her some more before there could be a hope of getting out. She told herself the voice didn't frighten her, that it was just lying and trying to trap her. So she pretended she wasn't scared, making jokes, light ones; then when it seemed like that wasn't working, Mira began trying to derange the place, pulling out its veins, its wires, its cords, but that only kept her there tighter. It started the whole day over again. That place had ways of keeping her there beyond her hopes of getting out.

The thing she had been trying to tell them was that psychology was the wrong thing to look into; that what they had to return to was looking at the surface. Even as she said it, her screams were echoing in her ears. *We have completely lost sight of the surface, and how useful it is to read the surface, and when we try to read what's underneath, we are just making up what's underneath.* Is that why she was brought here, trapped here and punished? Something about not believing the stories about the reality of what is underneath? But that wasn't the way she didn't believe it. She knew there was an underneath, but maybe they were saying, *No you didn't, you forgot how real is what's underneath.* She had forgotten the power of what's underneath; how it was strong and could tow you beneath it, and ultimately it could keep you there, so even Annie couldn't hear you, wherever Annie was. But Mira hadn't meant it that way! But maybe she had. Now she was confused about the surface and the underneath.

Then suddenly a square of light came into the leaf and broke it open from the middle, and the gold of the sun streamed along the path of its veins, so that life was bursting instead of expiring, and Mira fell out, out, out of a leaf.

Then she heard her father say, *Now my daughter is somewhere else, and if this side of the universe has something to say to her, I will hide from it what she did, and I will reply "I" for the both of us.*

FOUR

Annie and Mira were trying to talk to each other, so they took their cups of tea and went and sat at the bottom of a stairwell, and later they were walking down the street because Annie wanted a treat, so they stopped in a chocolate shop and spent a long time looking through the glass-topped counter, to figure out which chocolates to share. Annie wanted one which was dove grey and clear and in the shape of a crystal, about the size of a crab apple. She said she'd always wanted to try one of them, cut with facets and beautiful. But then Mira saw the woman putting some onto a tray and she called Annie over and showed her that it wasn't a hard crystal candy, like Annie had imagined; it was jiggly like Jell-O, and there was nothing special or magical about it at all.

Then they went inside and sat down at a little round table. Mira felt close to Annie. Even if they weren't as close as two people could possibly be, still they were sitting at the very same table, and that was pretty good. It didn't have to be as close as possible for it to be something good. She knew there were other people who Annie had taken to this shop, sharing a box of nine chocolates with.

Mira had been imagining that she was going to be in the leaf forever. She had thought that was what her body was now—

and that that was what her life was now—nothing to be shaken off. She had almost forgotten what it was like to not be in a leaf. Then Annie came and pulled her out. Annie had asked her if she wanted to get chocolates. Annie had realized Mira was in a leaf, but it had taken her a while to see it. She had seen Mira, without understanding. Then, after many months, she finally understood what she had seen; there, in the leaf, was Mira.

Annie wanted to tell her, and she did, *What happened is that you went into a leaf.* Annie told her everything she saw, without trying to talk her out of it. She didn't say, *You can be in a leaf for as long as you want to,* but she also didn't say, *You shouldn't remain in a leaf.* She just told Mira what she saw; that Mira had gone into a leaf. *You are seeming very green these days, and very still, and I wonder where your feelings are.* Annie had said this very gently, her lips close up against the leaf, like she was kissing it, and her breath was like kissing, and her breath tickled Mira a little bit. And Mira had the sense of rustling to life, as though feeling her body for the first time, and hearing what a human voice sounded like for the first time in so long.

There was the breath of Annie upon her, which made a shudder go through her; then Mira began to shudder to life, and she saw what she was missing, and she saw how she had missed it. Even though she had been happy to be so far away, she realized she had missed it. She was missing something. She could have slept away the rest of her days, feeling nothing, seeing nothing. It was becoming a cozy home. Why did she want all those feelings again, when feelings and people had become so difficult? But feelings and people were not so difficult. People loved her, or some of them did, or Annie did, perhaps. She must have loved her, for no one else had come to find her in the leaf and shake her out of it. *It's time*, said a little, ringing voice. But just as she hadn't been ready for her father to die when she had learned that he was ill, so she hadn't been ready to go back into the world again. She felt too tired for it. She didn't want to be roused. She wanted to be left alone. It was a nice place to be, in the leaf. She was with her father. She didn't want the company of other people, who meant nothing to her in comparison. She wanted only to be down by the water, or wherever her father was. He had died, and Mira had seen that he had gone to a good place, where he didn't have to be a person, and that there was nothing to fear in death; and so, without fear, she went there. She had followed him there. But how could she stay there with Annie rustling her branches, as she had done? Mira saw her beautiful face, which was the face of the person who had come to save her. It was a brave thing for Annie to do, to interrupt her in the leaf, where she would have been content to stay. But she wouldn't have been content to stay there forever. Even without the love of Annie, she would have eventually felt it was time to get out.

~

Annie said she wanted to try one of those big, dove-grey crystal sweets, and Mira said she would try one of the truffles, and when Annie was sitting at the table, Mira called her *Mom* by accident, turning around at the counter and calling out to her, *Mom!* Then Mira laughed and tried to cover it by explaining, *Oh, I'm just looking at these chocolates that have* Mom *written on them.* And she half-looked to see if there were any that said *Mom* on them, and indeed there were a few. Annie had pulled her out of the sleepy spell of death, and Mira said she wanted to drink rose-scented tea. They were going to have tea, cookies and chocolate, but not the beautiful dove-grey crystal candy that Annie originally had in mind. Annie had realized it was better to look at them than to have them, which is true of some things in this world.

Sitting opposite Annie, Mira now wondered if this was also true of herself and Annie, that sometimes a person is meant to move forward in the world with the one they love at a distance, and that the distance is there to make it more beautiful. To find the right distance from everything in life is the most important thing. To stand at the right distance, like God standing back from the canvas—for you can't see anything if you're too up close, and you can't see anything if you're too far back. So that is how she sat with Annie, there in the chocolate shop, across from her at the table. From across the table, Annie had managed to pull Mira back into life—back into this human life.

Then they walked down the street with its brick buildings and its concrete buildings and the concrete ground beneath them, with the sky up above them, and a dark shadow on the street on which they were walking. They had come from the stairwell outside of Annie's place, where they had been sitting on the steps, and Mira had forgotten her cup of tea there, but Annie had brought hers, so they would have to go into some place together. There were lots of places they could go, and Annie invited Mira to go with her somewhere.

Mira had forgotten that Annie was kind in that way: she had an innocence that wasn't even given to the innocent. Mira had forgotten how fragile Annie was. She had forgotten which of them was the orphan; which of them had everything, and which of them had nothing at all. This was partly the fault of the world they occupied—the ordinary world of that sort of forgetting. Annie was the one who had never had parents. For her, a building in a grey and very large city was the only mother and father she knew, dusty and dreary, with sheets too thin and her toes sticking out. While Mira had been tucked into bed every night by her father, and she had been told the most beautiful stories—of love, princesses, golden balls, wells, transformation, and frogs—stories that her father had made up, at her eager bidding. While Annie had had to make up her own stories, and she wasn't very good at it. Sometimes the stories Annie told herself went on and on, and they became too dark along the long, thin rope that she was following, and there was no one to gently lead her back. So how had she been able to lead Mira back? Annie knew about the dangers of going out so far that you could no longer find your way back. She saw that this was happening to Mira, so she helped her wind up the string of her story. It was a gentle winding and tying it up and handing it back to Mira, for Mira to do what she liked with it. It was the kind of soft white string they used to tie up those thin cardboard boxes at bakeries. Annie handed it back to Mira, and Mira understood, after leaving Annie that day—

and after the nine chocolates they shared—that she could un-ravel it if she wanted to, and even unravel it in the exact same way. But she kept it in her pocket, and her fingers opened its tangles softly, then bunched the string up tight again, but after a while she didn't even want to do that. Mira soon grew nau-seous touching it; it was too much to have it in her pocket all the time. So she put it in the teacup on her desk, the string that Annie had shown her.

FIVE

~

Are you sad to be living in the first draft—shoddily made, rushed, exuberant, malformed? No, you are proud to be strong enough to be living here now, one of God's expendable soldiers in the first draft of the world. There is some pride in having been created to make a better world come. There is some pride in being the ones who were made to be thrown out.

There is something exciting about a first draft—anarchic, scrappy, full of life, flawed. A first draft has something that a second one has not.

Our lives are full of misery, but what about the thrill of being here together, in this terrible time, knowing that life will not be so terrible once the next draft comes? They will be missing something that we have in this life, which we cannot even take joy in having, for we do not believe a world will ever come in which the particular suffering of ours will be gone.

Will there be any begetting in the next world? Will there be any romance? Or will people just hang around forever and love a universe that is so pure and so good that no one needs children in order to know what love is? How strange and sad our world will seem to them then—if they even find out about it— that we once had to create people with our own bodies, in order for there to be, among the billions of people already living, someone who could love us, and someone we could love in return. In the next draft of existence, everyone will love everyone, and they will consider our lives and think with a shudder, *Until they pushed a person out of their dirtiest parts, they had no one they could truly love, and no one who could truly love them—except for their own parents, who also pushed them out of their dirtiest parts.*

How crude and bizarre our world will seem to them then! How small, tragic and imperfect, when they consider what we had to do to find love.

Yet we can see what's beautiful in it. We can see the beauty, in a way they will never understand. They will not understand it, in the next draft of the world, which will be so much more utterly whole. Could any of us even bear that wholeness, us creatures of the first draft? Wouldn't we find something discomforting about such an excellent world?

Here we are, just living in the credits at the end of the movie. Everyone wants to see their name up on a screen. And whoever wants it is capable of putting it there. That is the work we are doing collectively now: just putting our names up on a screen. We have been given the technology for this one minor thing, here at the very end of the world, this one consolation, this booby prize.

～

I would like to come back after my death and see—
    What?
    Whether my works were kept by humanity. Whether my art is being exhibited fifty, seventy-five, a hundred years from now.
    So you want to return to earth to google yourself?
    Yes. Immortality means googling yourself forever.

Then the days became very dark. Trees were silhouetted against the sky and people on bicycles biked darkly past. They got drunk and biked through a terrible downpour.

There were downpours and there was heat—such terrible heat! It went on and on endlessly, like a bad older brother sitting on your face. We lay beneath our brothers and sweated. Who knew that the world would become so hot, when once it was cool, and life just beginning?

Back then, the fresh cool air felt like the beginning of something special. Adam and Eve in their Garden of Eden enjoyed a nice spring chill. They were both a little chilly, and the animals were too, and the air was as cold as glass. The air was very clear back then, back at the beginning of time. There weren't all these particles of dust floating everywhere; dust on top of everything from the centuries and the millennia. At the beginning of time, there was no dust. The flecks of skin from every human who has ever lived have been swept beneath so much furniture, under so many rugs, for millennia upon millennia. And yet the dust goes nowhere! It is all around us. It is hard to imagine how light and free the leaves in the trees once were, and how happy were the birds. We walk through our days in the dust of the dead. Two minutes out of the shower and already we are filthy. It is too disgusting to discuss.

We lived suspended in a soup, a depression so narrow and so deep we didn't even recognize we were feeling it. There was a horrible stasis in the air and our lives. We stood still in the stillness of time. It was like being in a plane that was slowly twirling to the ground. Did you look at the other people, or did you not look? Did you hold someone's hand and tell them, *I love you*, even if you'd only just met? Or did you squeeze your eyes shut and think of your loved ones, or think about your past, or pray? We were scuttling between these strategies like little bugs—sometimes praying, sometimes squeezing our eyes shut, sometimes thinking about the past, and sometimes saying *I love you* to a person we'd only just met—as civilization twirled all the way down. And apparently all the water had plastic in it, even the safe water that came in plastic bottles.

Were we the lucky ones, to have been chosen to live in this terrible time—to have been chosen to live in this heartbreaking time—as any moment in human civilization will break your heart, but none more so than the end?

How lonely it was at the end of the world, not to have all the people who lived before us, with us here to share it. We wanted them to return to this moment. We understood why, in apocalyptic tales, the bones of the dead rolled over the face of the earth, and everyone who ever lived was gathered in one place. Simply because the living wants the company of the dead. We want our ancestors to help us. We are scared. We want their company, and we want them to see it, as a dying father wants his loved ones close, gathered near the foot of his bed. So we wish for everyone who ever lived to be here with us, as the world we were all part of finally comes to an end. We feel they have the right to see it, to be here for the final day. Every human who ever lived is part of this draft which is now ending, so everyone who ever lived should be assembled when the curtain comes down.

How will people of the next draft think about this first draft—if they even retain a memory of it? They will remember this first draft the way we remember our first loves. The second draft will be like a mature love: long-lasting, decent, steady and right. It will not be like a first love: short-lived, painful, directionless and all wrong. They will look back on the world in which we are living with a certain bewilderment and awe, not quite believing that life was ever this way, just as when we are in a mature relationship, we can't ever believe we lived through that first one. Some part of us will always love the first one, and long for it a little bit. So will people in the next draft of existence hold within the deepest core of their beings a knowledge of this first draft—chaotic, dirty, dangerous and wrong—so different from the beautiful world that they will one day inhabit.

~

Or perhaps we don't really long for our first loves, despite all the songs and stories that tell us we do. Perhaps we are simply training the human soul for the even deeper longing it will one day feel, when it will sense, in some secret, small core of its being, the presence of this first draft of creation, and will confusedly long to return to it, as imperfect as it was.

Perhaps the human soul is in training for a longing it will never escape, once people are settled in the next draft of creation. That place will be better in so many ways—in all the ways that count. It will be bliss compared to this world we've been given, squatting here like teenagers in a house with painted cocks.

But just as those future people can never return to this draft, so we can never recapture the world we lived in with our first loves. So it will be for God in the next draft, when he will dream darkly about our world. He will not actually wish he could be here with us, but he will sense that the past had some extra vitality which the present does not.

SIX

Now Mira worked in a jewellery store, in the section of jew-elled rings. There were pink amethysts cut into the shapes of ovals and squares, tiny pears and teardrops, all bright and sweating. Minuscule diamonds were pressed into gold settings in the shape of half-moons, and sparkling. There was white gold, pink gold, and gold in deepening shades of yellow, and icy platinums which held within them a deep and private blue-ness. Mira sat and gazed at these rings all day. An elegant ci-trine, cut with thirty-six angles in the shape of a rectangle, was surrounded by tiny white pearls; it sat on the finger bulbously, robust as a miniature egg. Watermelon tourmalines with their bands of red shading into green were just asking to be sucked like candy, a different flavour on each end. Some rings were enamelled in the palest orange or an extravagant green. In the corner of a man's ring, made from black opal, was carved the shape of a falling star.

Mira guarded these bright fruits which had been dug out from the centre of the earth to sit on black velvet, pulsating. Then in would come a lady, with fingers thick and wrinkled, to put a heavy jewel on, or a woman with slim and listless fingers, too weak to hold but the smallest gem, and the essence of the beauty would vanish from the ring, once it was on a finger.

While the best of her classmates wrote for the magazines, Mira stayed in the very same place, anchored to the shop, mesmerized by midnight-blue, arrogant little sapphires. Any of the professors who had known her from her school days would have been unsurprised to find Mira sitting there, hunched behind the counter of a shop.

~

Then one day, she read in the newspaper that Matty was dead. It had been a horrible accident. They had found his car in the water, and Matty sitting in his car.

Reading the obituary, penned by his wife and two children, it was clear from their tone and the stories they told that Matty had been a bear all along. Of course, in one's teenage years, few are recognized as a bear, for they haven't yet chosen who to live for. In the middle years of life, Matty worked diligently in his father-in-law's hardware store. He had not shook the world as a critic.

That day, all the hard jewels looked like water. Mira's chest felt completely empty for him. In the afternoon, she was made to sell a fiery ruby, framed by forty diamonds. When she refused, her boss brought over the lady from watches, and Mira waited as the old man put it on his card: sixty thousand dollars.

In the middle years of life, you no longer have access to culture the same way you did before. You are mostly shut out. The party is happening behind a closed door. You can barely hear the party, and the scraps of conversations you can overhear are not the entire story. There is no pleasure in detecting only a few sounds through the wall. It's not that the young people have shut you out, so don't go envying the young people, who aren't even having that good a time of it. Just because they look great, doesn't mean they feel great.

God doesn't want the criticisms of the most dynamic parts of culture coming from someone in the middle of life, so the heart of culture is made invisible to you. But when God blinds your eyes to culture, he opens your eyes to everything else. But what else is there? Seasons, birds, the wind in the trees. So don't go chasing your old forms of sight. Instead, learn to see newly. Right now it may feel like a loss of sight, or like you don't understand the things you do see, but there is still a lot to see here. God doesn't care what you think about a *band*. God has put a hole in your head so things like that fall out of it. Yet you keep trying to put things like that into it! There is not a hole in your head for no reason at all. There is a hole in your head for certain things, and not for certain other things. Find the things that don't leak out and fill your head with those ones.

Midway through life, the gods strip us. Take anything real that happens in the middle of life; the decline of the body, the death of one's friends, the loss of a job, a strange sense of time. All these things are evidence that one is being stripped. The gods strip us of our parents, our ambitions, our friendships, our beauty—different things from different people. They strip some people more and others less. They strip us of whatever they need to in order to see us more clearly.

One's thoughtless marriage at twenty-five is perhaps forgivable in light of youth, but in the moment of being stripped, we are looked at as though our actions were undertaken by a person who is ageless and complete. Stripped of the glamour and beauty of youth, everything we ever did—it all looks different now. We can see our choices as acts in themselves, not stages on life's way, for if progress in human history is an illusion, so is progress in a human life.

~

In the moment of being stripped, a person becomes more clear to themselves. We can see our defects and limitations in a way we never could before. There is a new orientation to life and the self when the eyes of the gods are upon you.

The few moments of real presence you have ever felt in your life might mean that a god was inside someone near you, using them to see you. The few moments of real insight we've ever had about another might indicate that a god was inside us at that moment, using us to see them. When they brighten the characteristics of another person, it is like turning on a light in a darkened room. We might remember that moment of seeing better than any of the other moments in our lives.

The person who the gods are watching through you often develops a certain attachment to you. That person may find themselves thinking about you a lot, and you may find yourself thinking about them a lot, too. It often happens between two such people that they will feel fated to be in each other's lives. They might like or dislike the other one, or have no clear feelings between them at all, yet there they are, for minutes or hours or weeks or years, mysteriously in each other's orbit, as though something of significance is going on.

Then, when the desire suddenly comes over a person to swiftly and dramatically change their life, it is often a desire to evade the eyes of the gods. It may feel like something threatening is happening—something dangerous from which they must escape. A person might blame this feeling on the choices they made, or grow certain that they could create a better life than the one they're living now. They might blame the person who the gods have inhabited for all of their discomforts, so they try to flee their literal home. Some people move to a smaller town, or seek out someone they loved before, and try to be with them again. Bachelors wish to get married, and married people wish to get a divorce; to make one last bid for the excellent life they feel that they deserve.

But the gods who are watching you from inside another one don't disappear if you flee your life. They will leave the body of your child, your neighbour, or your friend—whoever they have inhabited to watch you—and find a body in your new life to inhabit, and continue to watch you from there.

The gods sometimes take the form of a bacteria or virus, and often that's what an illness is—just a swarm of invading gods. Then part of what's so exhausting about being ill is that you have been invaded by the gods. They are using your body to watch someone near you, to see what humans are like in this draft of the world, so they can make them better in the next one.

The gods sometimes kill the bodies of the people they enter. They tell themselves they make people sick to dying to judge those who gather around the dying one, to see how they behave in such a critical situation. But really it's because they haven't figured out a reliable way of exiting someone's body without inadvertently killing them.

The week that Mira was being stripped of her father, she felt the gods inside him, watching her. That is when she saw herself truly: that she had loved art and books more than she had loved her own father. The gods took note of this, then they fled.

How Mira hated being a bird in this draft of creation. How she wished, like her father, she had been born a bear!

~

Mira felt bad. If she could undo the past, she would do it. She had missed the opportunity for so much time with him. She had hurt her father and deprived herself.

But did she want to undo the past because she had lived it wrongly, or was regret just a bug in how she'd been made? The most important thing about her, for God, was her critical impulse—her desire to undo things. It was the thing inside her that mattered most. But this undoing impulse made her suffer. When she thought back on her life with her father, she wanted to remember their laughter, his spirit, his kindness, all the ways she had been good to him, and everything loving and fine. Why could the beauty his death had shown her not be stronger than her wish to change the way that things had been before?

He had not wanted to tell Mira that he was near to dying, because he wanted her to keep living her life. But he also wanted her close, and it wasn't always possible for him not to be upset that she wasn't with him more often, especially the year he was dying. She had wanted to be close, and to spend more time together, but something in her had also kept her away, more than maybe was right. But it felt important and like it had to be done—to remain out in the world without him, as though a repetition of the demands of the past, when she had tried to keep a distance or else risk falling into their twinned well forever. He agreed that he wanted this— for her to be out in the world without him. Both of them wanted the very same thing—for the other one to be living their own life—but they also wanted to be close and to be living the same one.

She had found it hard to be near him that final year, blinders on both of their eyes; neither of them wanting to see the coming end of it. He had felt bad about wanting her to stay, then immediately wishing for her to return, and she felt guilty about wanting to go. But she brought back for him everything good in the world that she found there; caramels in silver-and-blue foils. But she did not always return with presents, for she was afraid of becoming his wife. She had loved the feeling that existed between them when she was a little girl, and he would tell her stories about three grown brothers who had set off into the world, each of them seeking their own treasure, and each returning home with something special they found, answering the riddle their father had posed to them in their own, unique way. What was the riddle that Mira had been sent out into the world to answer? Maybe, *What is the actual distance of love?*

~

Then all of this remembering made Mira feel tired, like she had the year her father was dying, sitting with him in his own house, some strange narcotic coursing through her veins, sending her deeply into sleep, and deeply into yawning, one yawn following the next, the heaviest narcotic she had ever known, talking there on the couch with him, while the weight of that year was as suffocating as sleep. *Why don't you take a nap on the couch*, he would ask her, and she would say no, she had to go home. She couldn't let herself fall asleep on his couch in that house of death and dying, although she once fell asleep on his couch, and when she woke up, her heart felt as bright as that of a clear-hearted child. He was watching television with the headphones on. It had been so nice to wake up near him, in his own home.

This was the entirety of the life they shared, in the first draft of their existence together.

~

She remembered the way he would wave good-bye to her from his doorstep, and he would not turn around to go back inside until she was halfway up the block, out of the sight of his failing eyesight, and even somewhat past it.

The frail back of her father in his tricolour jersey, and his khaki pants. The thinness of her father, and feeling the bones in his back as she hugged him, every bone in his spine, and the patchy scratching of his ill-shaven cheek whenever she kissed him hello. And when she took down the painting over the TV, clearing out his house the month after he died, the square of the wall beneath the painting was pulsating slightly in the shape of a heart, like the house really did love her, because of how much her father did, who had sat there facing the wall of his living room, loving her every day of his life.

It is easy to feel love for one's child. Nothing on earth is easier. A father often has a special love for a daughter. It is natural to want to shine your interest and pride onto your own child. It is simple to love one's own creature. But that is a debt the child can never repay—to have been given all that love and care. It feels completely unbalanced.

There is a ruthlessness to life. It seems to lack balance—and in its particulars, it does. None of us is able to stand far back enough from life to see the balance that somehow exists. The child is never who the parent wants them to be, and they must not be. Even if a daughter accepts the lessons of her father, she will turn into a creature he didn't expect. But that is entirely necessary. That is how the world changes, how values and criticisms evolve and change. A child must follow the rules of her own being. A parent can never truly understand what those values or rules are. A child is an alien to the parent, which hurts the parent a little. The child's whole life can feel like a betrayal. But life is not a betrayal of life.

The parent should not feel betrayed, but in the smallness of time, a parent does. A daughter might feel guilty for having her own laws, but life will force her to live them. This was also the case for her parent; she thinks she is the first one to suffer this way, but she is not. Not every parent knows in advance that being a parent will mean this eventual pain; that the most important thing for you will not be the most important thing for your child. This is something the child suffers from, too.

The parent thinks the child should do something to fix it, but this is against life, so the child cannot. The child suffers from this, too. No daughter made up the rules of life, which has its own laws, like her parent does; and like she does, too. For instance, that a daughter must leave her father and go off into the world. The daughter didn't make this up. It happens through the body. The body becomes a woman and it cannot turn back.

~

Mira felt that her father would have liked her to marry him. But even if she wanted to, she couldn't have done it. It is one of the most important things that life does not allow. Perhaps because the parent wants it. So life must not allow.

Should the child feel guilty over what life does not allow? No, the child is naturally aligned with life against what the parent desires, so the child has more power, and so she feels guilty, for having so much power. More right, it seems, would be the other way around.

What unnatural thing has Mira done to wrest so much power away from her father? Nothing. It is the natural thing that life wanted, and so it made her do it, whispering, *Go into the world and find someone else to love. While your father is alone and crying. Stop always thinking about your father, who is alone and crying at home.*

Perhaps now that he is dead, she can marry her father. Mira spontaneously had this thought, then she went into a leaf. Then Annie drew her out again.

SEVEN

Annie had moved to a small town, to work with groups of people, to help them repair their collective delusions. Mira had heard the rumours, and she became confused and upset when she learned that this was what Annie was doing. It had been some time since they had last seen each other, when Annie drew Mira out of the leaf, but Mira still thought about her often. When Mira had felt the wisdom of the universe all around her, she had learned that a fixer was the wrong thing to be, and she felt it was important to tell Annie. She didn't think Annie was going to be punished for becoming a fixer, but she didn't want her to waste her life.

Mira thought she understood what Annie was hoping to do as a fixer in that small town: humans brought in fixers because they couldn't stand it. Fixers had their own ideas about things; about relationships and the psyche and the world of people, and what it meant to be in a family, and that families were perverse. They made up stories, meddling in the structure that had been given to humans, as old as a tree. Fixers were like the gardeners of the family, trimming back its branches. But did a family need a gardener to trim it down?

~

It is natural for a person to want to fix things, but we can't fix the way we think we can, by actually becoming fixers. If anyone muddles with creation, God muddles it back again. Any change that seems hopeful and improving—if it was a person who made it—will soon be muddled back by God, who jealously wants to do the fixing.

Annie had grown up in an orphanage, so perhaps she had never learned this. Annie needed someone in her family to help her. Who was Annie's family? Mira thought, *I am.*

So she decided to go and visit her in her new home.

It was a beautiful fall day when Mira moved from the city with her boxes containing all of her things. As she drove, in whatever direction she looked, there was a blazing red tree, or a wistful yellow one, and there were many trees that were buoyantly green, and others that had leaves which were orange and bright, and not one of the leaves had yet fallen on the ground, brittle and dry. There were no fallen leaves, the colour of sidewalk. Mira's part of the world was experiencing three months of the slowest and most luxurious fall, and there was no rushing towards winter. Winter would come in its own time. Mira knew that leaves were one of a tree's best reasons for being. She drove past billions of leaves, trillions of them, whole universes of leaves; more leaves than there had ever been people. She whipped past all of them in her tiny yellow car.

As she drove, she remembered one of the first times she had been deeply stirred, standing before Manet's *Asparagus*. It was the simplicity of his expression, the lightness of his touch, the muteness of his colours, how minor a thing an asparagus is, and his name like a beautiful leaf in the corner. It was the perfect balance between carefulness and carelessness, and the delicate and unassuming heart he put into every line. She knew then that she would always be drawn to his paintings—in any museum in the world.

Mira knew that humans made art because we were made in God's image—which doesn't mean we look like God; it means we like doing the same thing God likes. Both making life and making art are pouring spirit into form.

~

Now she wondered, *What if, when Manet died, the life that was in him left his body and entered a pig that was being led down the road? And what if some of Manet's spirit went into the doctor who was standing near?* Would these departed spirits, through some force of magnetism, ever find each other again? Did a spirit which once lived in a body contain something that, even if it was split into a thousand pieces and separated for a hundred years, if those pieces came close in separate bodies, could draw those bodies near?

What if some of the spirit that had been in Manet travelled through pigs and plants and people until some of it wound up in Mira, and this was why she was so drawn to his paintings—because spirits draw their related parts close, like orphans seeking their kin.

An artist is driven to make art by the spirit inside them, making an artwork like a signal or flare calling out, beckoning its kin to come near. This is why an artist never tires of their task. A bird finds it hard to attend to one person, and this is the reason why: because they have a desperate need—to create an aesthetic surface to put between themselves and the world, to make the spirits whole. Then how well can we expect a bird to love, when they are daily applying their love to a surface? While a bear isn't driven to love through a surface: they join with other creatures much more directly.

And what is love like for a fish? This is what Mira was anxiously wondering as she drove wildly in her yellow car to the small town where Annie was now living.

Mira crouched in the garden, outside a room at the back of Annie's house, where Annie was meeting with twenty people, who sat on the floor and in chairs, as if they were in group therapy or at a union meeting. Mira could see only the back of Annie's head.

The room might have once been used as a greenhouse: it was entirely made of windows, and even the pointed roof was iron and glass. The room had three statues in it, each the size of a tall, thin child: one of a fish, one of a bird, and one of a bear. They had been carved out of black-veined, bluish-grey marble.

Mira hid there, her feet held tightly by the branches and the brambles and the ivy she'd stepped in. Annie was talking to the group, who were gazing up at her quietly. They sat around on pillows, or on the floor, or on wicker chairs against the walls; sometimes one of them spoke, sometimes several did, but mostly they listened to Annie. Mira watched quietly until the meeting was over, and the people of the town went into the hallway, making for the front door. When Annie left the room, after the last one had gone out, Mira pulled herself out from the brambles, cursing as she cut her thumb on a vine.

As she walked along the side of the house to the front, she

peered in most of the windows. Annie's house was lovely. There was sunlight pouring in from every direction, lots of plants and wooden floors, and colourful throw pillows and woven rugs. It was beautiful and nothing like Annie. The people in that small town must have been grateful that she was coming to help them, and believed that she really could, so they had given her this elegant home, and even put her name on a wooden plaque, and stuck it into the front lawn.

～

Passing by an open garbage can, Mira looked inside it. Against the side of a clear plastic bag, she noticed a few bottles of caffeine pills. Mira knew what this meant. People complained of being tired, exhaustion, not realizing that this was put in them so they wouldn't do as many things. Such people railed against their fatigue—the ones who were determined to fix things. In order to stop them, the gods tired them out. The weariest people are being the most prevented. They are the most dangerous ones, who would change the world if they could. We know which people are threatening to the gods by how exhausted they feel all the time. Those who would not make as many fixes are not given as much fatigue. You know the gods consider you dangerous if you are tired all the time.

When Annie opened the door to Mira that night, Mira thought that Annie looked different from how she had looked all those years before. She wore sort of professional clothes, the colour of a rotting fish, and the skin on her face was scaly and dry, and her brownish eyes had grown even darker; a black-and-gold flecked stone.

Mira stood on her doorstep, as drawn to her as she had ever been. Annie welcomed her in, and they went and sat at her kitchen table, and Annie served her tea that was too strong for Mira to drink it.

~

Mira began telling Annie what she knew, about how we are here to follow the family traditions with faith, and that in order for people to follow the traditions, it is important to keep the fixers out. That a family is a structure given to humans, as old as a tree, while fixers are like the reckless gardeners, sawing off the branches.

Annie listened politely, with a face of cold marble. Then she told Mira that she had it all wrong: it would have been impossible for Mira to receive the universe's wisdom if, when she did, she was in a leaf with her father. It would have been her *father's* wisdom, or the wisdom of the universe as filtered through her father, and don't forget, her father was a bear. *I think you are mistaking the word "family" for the word "familiar." It is the familiars we were put on earth to find, who might or might not be our family. It is the "familiars" we must attend to—but cautiously, not with faith.*

Hearing this caused a thud inside Mira's chest. What Annie was saying couldn't be more clear. Annie, who was a fish, found everyone familiar—no one person more or less than the next. For Annie, Mira was like anyone who might visit her in her home. Yet Annie had, from the start, been uniquely familiar to Mira, which felt like something special. Annie stood apart from the rest, lit by a special beauty. But how could she explain this to Annie?

Hoping and intending for Annie to be moved, Mira said, *I just want to help you, because I consider you my family.* She reached her hand across the table in a tentative way.

Instead of sighing or beginning to cry, Annie frowned. *People should care for other people because they are familiar— because they're also humans—not because they're family.*

Mira grew silent. Maybe Annie was right. She had thought she loved her father because he was family. But that was the reasoning of a bear! She didn't think she'd loved him because he was human. Was it because she had found his spirit beautiful? She couldn't become distracted.

I still think it's wrong to be a fixer, Mira said.

That's rich for you to say!—you, who have never tried to fix anything!

189

~

They talked like this, with increasing difficulty, until around midnight, when the bird in the cuckoo clock spun crazily out of its brown wooden door. Then Annie said she was tired, although she didn't look so tired, but maybe she'd had enough of Mira.

Mira left, certain she had handled the night poorly. What she had really wanted, she now saw, was for Annie to admit that she loved her. The idea that Mira had come to warn Annie against being a fixer had just been an excuse. She had been lying to herself in the car, and so she hadn't been honest with Annie, and so the whole conversation had gone badly. The entire evening had been a mistake.

Mira had spent so much of the second half of her life thinking about people from the first half—her father and Annie—who she felt she never should have abandoned. Yet none of the jewels that had sparkled back then had she been able to draw with her down through time. She couldn't let it go! What were one's middle years—with its laziness and perspective—*for*, besides sweeping up the glittering jewels of the past, and gathering them near to one now? She could see so clearly what had been the jewels. They sparkled so brightly against the dark night of her history, no way to deny them.

~

If Mira returned to the earth in a million hot years, she would have to remember to hold close the jewels from the first half of her life, so she wouldn't have to spend the second half going off in search of them.

But was this a promise to remember—or a promise to forget? For a person would never sparkle in the second half of life, the way they had sparkled for you in the first. Because once the watching gods have left a person, they never return to that person again, to watch who they were watching before. And it is their watching that creates the sparkle, the meaning, the implant in the mind. Being together would not feel the same if it was missing those observant little gods, collecting information for the next draft of the world.

When Mira met Annie in the second half of life, the hours they spent together were not being collected as material for the making of a future world. It was just two people hanging out together—which was fine, as far as it went.

Returning to her rented bungalow in the early hours of the morning, Mira realized that the roof was smoking. Flames of orange were going up, and a fire truck had come. Neighbours were standing in the street, and the blue-and-red lights of a police car were turning round and round. One of the firemen asked Mira, before heading inside, if there was anything that needed saving. Mira's mind went blank. What did she even *own*? She said, *I don't think there's anything.* So the fireman went inside.

When they finally emerged from the house, the one who had spoken to Mira came and explained that the floors were now damp: it had been tar, friction, and something else in the roof that had set off sparks between the wires, and now everything would smell like smoke: her clothes would, her bed would, and so would all the linens. The fireman said she should check into a hotel, and return for her things in the morning. So she went inside to get her pajamas and her toothbrush. She roamed through the dark and smoky house, and saw the huge muddy prints of their rubber-booted feet. Then she noticed a caved-in cardboard box. She had left it on the floor, not yet unpacked. One of the firemen had stepped in it. When Mira leaned down to open it up, she found her lamp was totally mangled. She let the red and green stones fall through her hands.

Of course she would have wanted to save the lamp! But when she had been asked what she wanted to save, she had forgotten everything. If everything else had also been ruined, perhaps she wouldn't be so upset, but that her lamp was the only thing, made it the best thing. Now she longed for its former condition. Why had she not unpacked it first, with the utmost reverence and care? Because as soon as she had arrived in Annie's town, she had immediately gone to see Annie. How could she have been so stupid? She had given no thought to this precious thing. How could she have ever forgotten that the lamp was better than anything?

～

Perhaps it won't be so bad when we all die at once, once the beginning to the second draft comes; perhaps it won't be so upsetting. That we are made to die, one at a time, here in the first draft of existence—that is the pain and the longing. That is the beautiful.

Now the snow was coming down from the ink-black sky, and there was the scent in the air of fresh snow air. The low moon was hidden behind several clouds. Mira was in the field beside the highway hotel, where she had moved the night of the fire. She was looking out through the fake fur of her hood, unable to see properly because the hood was too big and it kept falling over her eyes. Meanwhile, God was hearing her complaints. *My hood is too big, it keeps falling over my eyes.* And she had spent too much money on the coat! *And this coat cost too much. Why do I so wastefully spend money?* In the next draft of existence, there would be no coats, and there would be no money. So many of our complaints applied only to this draft, where the weather was such, and shame was such, that all these clothes were needed. It wouldn't necessarily be like that in the next draft of existence. But we didn't know what would be different in the next draft, or what would be the same, so we sent all our complaints up to God.

Mira wished she was noticing the beauty of the cool, thick cotton falling from the sky, and the branches hanging low with the heavy, wet snow. And she *was*, but not as much as she was feeling frustrated with her hood, and with having obviously made the wrong purchase. Why had she not waited for a better coat? Because she hated thinking about coats. Because she hated shopping. But a person born into this draft had the necessity of acquiring clothing. God knew this caused all sorts of frustrations, and hearing Mira's complaints, he knew it again. Mira walked through the parking lot, into the lobby, and up to her room, where she hung her damp coat in the closet and removed her winter boots by the door. Then she stepped into a puddle of snow, and now the bottom of her sock was wet. Now she had a complaint about her sock! Why was she here? Why did she *exist*? To complain to the creator about *socks*? Why had God not destroyed this draft, and started on a new one already? What was he waiting to *hear*?

Mira lay in bed as she thought back on her conversation with Annie, and about all the scenes of their youth—sitting on the floor of Annie's apartment, the peanut soup, their kiss in the street. She saw them there, two girls down below—as if even while living it, she had been up in the sky, at a distance. Why, she wondered, when she turned her mind to the past, did she never recall what happened through her own eyes, but from some vantage point higher up and further back—back behind her body, way above her head, a perch that would have been impossible to reach, floating in midair? Perhaps because the most crucial perspective on her life had never been hers at all.

That the most important viewpoint should belong to God, not people, made Mira really upset. Wasn't it cruel to make sensitive creatures, simply to serve your own ends, here in the first draft of existence? Yet even in the next draft, we will still be serving God's ends, as the grateful audience of his beautiful show. Then is it even *possible* to make creatures to serve their own ends, or will your ends always limit their freedom, if you are the one who made them?

Mira had never wanted what God, or her father, most wanted from her, and this had caused her so much pain. She had been unable to return the warm love of a bear. And she hated being a critic. She just wanted to feel the same happiness, appreciation, and beauty that she had felt when her father's spirit came into her. Yet even that feeling—that corrective desire—was the desire and wish of a critic.

~

How can a person disobey their God, the very God that made them? And what will happen if you disobey? Probably God will strike you dead. But what happens if your God dies before you? *Then* are you allowed to disobey? Can it even be called a disobedience, if there is no longer someone around with any idea of what it means for you to disobey? Why did it seem like the only way to live—was to disobey?

She would let any shame come upon her. She would wear the costume of a leaf. She wouldn't dress in pearls and satin. A leaf is dressed only by the snow and the rain. She would not give her opinion about anything. She would take no actions, and would remain in one place, like a leaf does, and when she died, she would fall to the ground. A leaf remains on the branch on which it's been grown, it does not change the world around it. She would not go into the world to critique or fix it. If she would be mocked for wearing her costume, she would not try to correct the people who mocked her. She did not think that everyone should be a leaf. She didn't think anyone should not be. She would not dress as a leaf to protest how others were living. She would not do it to be the best kind of person, or even the very worst one.

Of course, the whole idea was stupid! There could be no arguing her case before anyone. But being a leaf, she wouldn't have to. A leaf isn't called on to speak before judges. Naturally her costume wouldn't accomplish anything, but who expects a leaf to accomplish a thing? The best thing that a leaf can do is release a bit of oxygen into the air.

Mira bought some green fabric and some green thread and a silver needle, and she began to sew her costume. She mixed up green paint with her face cream, then she returned to sewing the leaf. It was wide around the middle, and pointed at both ends, with little veins that she traced in brown paint and a spine down the centre. One side of the costume would cover her front, the other would cover her back, and there was a space for her head to go through. The costume grew stiff as she filled it with rags. She pulled it on and pushed her arms through the holes in both of its sides. Then she went off in search of brown leotards and black sneakers, then she put them on.

She would look at the world only in order to love it—and everyone would hate her.

Annie answered the door to Mira and found her standing there in her leaf costume. The sun was shining, and the sky was bright behind Mira. Annie let her in and noticed her green hands, and said very quickly, *Please don't touch any of the furniture*. Perhaps Mira had been wrong to love Annie. But not loving her had not been within the realm of her choosing.

Mira followed Annie into the back room, and sat down on the wooden floor of the greenhouse, so she wouldn't stain the fabric of the very nice pillows and chairs. Then she began to cry. A few green tears ran down her cheeks and dripped onto her costume. She wiped her eyes, then her eyes started burning from the green paint which she had painted onto her hands, and her eyes began tearing up worse in pain. She decided she would go and find green gloves tomorrow, instead of painting her hands with green paint.

I'm sure you wouldn't want to be seen with me like this, at any of your important parties!

Of course I wouldn't, Mira.

Mira's heart began thumping. She had always known it. She had known it from the day they met, back in Annie's apartment, but she had always ignored it. Annie had not been made to love her. It was now hard for Mira to stand up from the floor, because she didn't want to stain it with her hands. Then she was a kneeling leaf. Then she managed to get to her feet in her very awkward costume.

Could Annie tolerate Mira as a leaf? Of course not. Mira had no sense or judgement. She'd never had! She was just a dumb bird, all instinct and flying. Annie led her to the front door and opened it, and stood on the threshold as Mira went out. Mira still loved Annie, and she loved the world—more than it even made sense to. She didn't want to criticize a bit of it.

Annie called out to her, *You should change!*

Does she mean I should change who I am, Mira thought, *or change out of my leaf costume, into my regular clothes?*

~

Mira walked off, looking down. She should have known that Annie's love would be withdrawn. All help always is. Mira should have known her father would be withdrawn. Whatever you depend on will be withdrawn, for when the gods are coming to strip you, they want to leave you with nothing.

Mira moved from that town, stripped of the hope she had so long carried, of one day finally having something good and lasting with Annie. She wore her leaf costume a little more. No one seemed to like it, but no one said so to her face. She wore it until it became too dirty, then she realized she didn't know how to clean it. So she hung it up.

EIGHT

One cool and cloudy afternoon, Mira returned to the lake where she had gone after her father had died. Walking there, she saw a seashell in the sand that seemed to call out to her. It had a knobby grey-and-green surface, like the shell of an ancient turtle that had been submerged in the water for a million hot years, then dragged itself onto the shore.

She picked it up, and the seashell seemed to speak to her, saying, *You will have so many more years of living, and the years will draw you far from this time when you feel so bad, and time will crust over everything, and so much more will happen to you, and though the present is all you have right now, it will all be far in the past one day, something from another time, like everything I have moved beyond, as an ancient seashell, I don't remember my youth, do you think that I do?—and the things I did when I was shiny and new, now I'm an old shell, like you will one day be, so take me with you as a reminder that this present moment will one day be gone, and its troubles buried beneath so many layers of living.*

Mira took the talking shell and put it in her pocket. Then she returned home, where she put it on her vanity with her jewels and her makeup.

~

Later, whenever she looked at it, Mira was reassured that it was only her imagination and her striving to obey that gave her those such-big feelings of remorse, which came out of her belief that things could be better than they were—as if not being able to bring to some beautiful conclusion her love for Annie, or not having been able to settle the right distance between her father and herself, were the only ways she had gone wrong; as if life was not a constant falling short of the many tasks that God, and others, and even we, have given ourselves.

It was a delusion to think she had created the world and everything in it; that she had made up its rules and was always to blame. Where had that idea come from? Or did everyone feel that way, a little bit, for it was actually God who was feeling it—the God who had *in fact* created the world, while we picked up on his shame for having made it, in some ways, poorly, and mistook his feeling of responsibility for our own.

That was why she needed that ugly old seashell; because it was the contour and shape of her insides. It was a reminder of what a human self was, and what a human life was: not a beautiful glass lamp just this side of being broken, or a lovely gold ring with a single dent in it. But a battered old seashell, formed over millions of years, made to endure.

Then Mira went about her days, buying a bag of pears at the grocery store, and she left her butter in a glass-topped dish on the counter, so it would be soft when she went to butter her toast. And in the winter, or in the rainy woods, she walked down steep hills with her feet turned sideways, the way her father had taught her.

NINE

Annie and Mira met once more, this time differently. This time it was Mira who was dying, and Annie had come with all the supplies, not just to Mira's house, but to the houses of the many who were suffering. She was surprised to find Mira on the floor; not surprised by the sight of a woman on the floor, or one who found her bedsheets too hot, but by the fact that it was Mira.

Sometimes it is the orphans, the fish—who were sent to swim alone in the world's cold waters—who see the whole picture most clearly. They have no parents blocking their sight, and swimming as they do, under the water, if they are not afraid to open their eyes, everything becomes incredibly clear.

Annie pulled Mira into her arms, and Mira recognized Annie. She hoisted her back into bed, then sat down at the edge of it. She let her other responsibilities go. There were other people who could take over for now. Annie had learned, over the past year, what it looked like when the end was near. Mira's hair was wet on her face, and her eyes didn't open so easily, but still she managed to smile, and Annie, unafraid, cradled Mira's head.

Mira was so glad that she had drawn Annie near. Perhaps this meant that Annie loved her, even if Annie didn't know it, for she might not have been the sort of person who could know it.

It was difficult for Mira to talk, but it felt better not to; just to be in bed with Annie, and for them to be touching—wasn't that what she had always wanted? And now here she was, and she got it. Life was always playing its tricks, never just giving, and never just taking away, but always both. Here again it was a situation of both, as the spirit fled Mira—through all the cells of her body.

The light in the room was dim, and as the day grew dark, a last stretch of blue came in through the window. For Mira, this blue might have been twenty years, it might have been thirty. Her entire life was just lying in that bed, her head in Annie's hands. Who knows how all of this seemed to Annie? What is this world to a fish?

Something happened to the soul of Mira's father the moment the life left her, a reawakening to what he had known in the moment of his own death; that everything on this earth is forgiven. He was not a bad father, and she was not a bad child, and there could be no badness between two such people who loved each other as they did. They had loved each other and so all was forgiven, for this draft is not just a place of blessings where things are supposed to go well. Getting through it is enough, and they did. They got through their entire lives to death. And the final moments are the true ones, and the true ones are the truest of all.

And this was all that was needed for them to—*good-night, sleep tight, don't let the bedbugs bite, if they do, pinch them till they're black and blue.* What are bedbugs? Just little bugs that live in a mattress. Are they real? Yes, but don't worry, I don't think we have bedbugs. Is there time for another story? No, sweetie, go to sleep. A glass of water? Here you go. Will you tell me one about a bird named Mira, who had a friend who was a beautiful fish, and you're in the story as a bear, and they all live together forever? Sure, I'll tell it to you tomorrow night. Okay, I love you. I love you. I love you! Go to sleep. I love you!

I love you. I love you! Could you please leave the door open a bit? Hey, where are you going? Nowhere, don't worry, I'll just be downstairs.